P9-CFC-243

Trino's Time

Diane Gonzales Bertrand

PIÑATA BOOKS
ARTE PÚBLICO PRESS
HOUSTON, TEXAS

This volume is made possible through grants from the National Endowment for the Arts (a federal agency), Andrew W. Mellon Foundation, the Lila Wallace-Reader's Digest Fund and the City of Houston through The Cultural Arts Council of Houston, Harris County.

Piñata Books are full of surprises!

Piñata Books

An imprint of
Arte Público Press
University of Houston
Houston, Texas 77204-2174

Cover illustration and design by Vega Design Group

Bertrand, Diane Gonzales.
　　Trino's Time / by Diane Gonzales Bertrand.
　　　p.　cm.
　　Summary: With the help of some friends and a Tejano hero that he discovers in history class, thirteen-years old Trino copes with his problems and his world.
　　ISBN 1-55885-316-2 — ISBN 1-55885-317-0 (pbk. : alk. paper)
　　[1. Mexican Americans—Fiction.]　I. Title.
　　PZ7.B46352 Tr 2001
　　[Fic]—dc21　　　　　　　　　　　　　　　　　　00-065257
　　　　　　　　　　　　　　　　　　　　　　　　　　　　CIP

♾ The paper used in this publication meets the requirements of the American National Standard for Information Sciences—Permanence of Paper for Printed Library Materials, ANSI Z39.48-1984.

1 2 3 4 5 6 7 8 9 0　　　　　　10 9 8 7 6 5 4 3 2 1

To my son,
Nicholas Gilbert Bertrand,
with love.

To Félix D. Almaraz, Jr., Ph.D.,
my favorite Texas history teacher

Chapter 1
Out on a Limb

One wrong step meant a broken neck. Or worse.

Trino's sweat trailed down his back as he inched across the big branch. Perched high in a rotting oak tree, he tried not to think about anything but that one cropped branch that had refused to fall to the ground. But he couldn't stop thinking about what he was doing.

He could just imagine the newsman on TV announcing, "Trino Olivares, age thirteen, died today when he fell out of a tree. He was only getting paid twenty bucks for the job. Wasn't he stupid, folks?"

What had ever made Trino say to Nick, "I'll climb up and shake it loose."

This was the second weekend Nick had asked Trino to work with him, earning extra money by trimming trees. So far, it had been long, hot work, but it hadn't been hard. Or very interesting. Just cutting, breaking, piling, loading, and hauling the branches to the city dump.

Finally, Trino had a chance to do something that could be fun.

"I can climb up there easy, Nick," Trino had bragged. "I'll climb up and shake it loose."

Nick had been dating his mom for a month now, and while Trino still didn't trust the guy, he had wanted Nick

1

to know that Trino had the guts to do anything that needed to be done. Even if it was a little dangerous.

"No, I should go," Nick had said. "If you fall out of a tree, your mother will kill both of us."

Trino wouldn't have minded if Nick got into trouble with his mom. "Come on, Nick. You know that you're too big to climb up there."

And he knew he had made sense. Nick Longoria was very tall and had a lot of strength. Trino had seen the man pull out a tree root with his bare hands. And he had guessed that Nick was around thirty, so Nick could probably climb the tree well enough. But Trino knew he was lighter, better suited to stand on an old branch.

"I can do it, Nick. Here."

And then Trino had handed over the pole with the branch trimmer and headed up the metal ladder. Only it didn't go up high enough. That's when he had to climb. And halfway up, scraping his hands and arms against the rough tree trunk, he had really started to sweat. His legs were protected by his jeans, but his worn-out shoes slipped off the natural dips, bumps, and stumps around the trunk. Sometimes, he could only use his arms to pull himself up, and the movements made his T-shirt rise, exposing his stomach to scrapes and tiny slashes of pain. But he couldn't do anything about it. Just keep climbing. He couldn't look like a wimp in front of Nick.

Only once did he look down, and heard Nick's deep voice say, "Don't look down. Keep your eyes on what's ahead of you."

Finally, Trino had gotten to a place where he thought he could stand on a steady branch and shake that dangling one loose. He raised one arm to grip the branch above him so he could walk upright. He inched closer to the tangle of branches, one of them already cut, but refusing to drop down. He wondered if guys who worked on telephone poles ever felt nervous.

One wrong step meant a broken neck. *Or worse.*

That's when he heard the cracking of wood under his right foot.

Trino stopped, his whole body stiff with fear. Slowly, he looked down at his feet, and from there beyond, far, far down to Nick's dark brown face, to his long body, to the nest of branches around his feet, to the hard grayish-brown dirt where he stood.

"What's wrong?" Nick called up.

Trino didn't dare speak, afraid the sound of his voice might crack the branch. He raised his eyes and looked ahead of him, silently cussing at the branch for not dropping like it was supposed to.

Suddenly he decided to ask for a raise. *Twenty-five dollars*, he would tell Nick. Provided he didn't fall out of the tree and break his neck first.

Trino looked up at the branch his hands circled. He tested its strength by pulling it towards him. It moved very little, so Trino squeezed his hands around it much tighter.

Slowly, he put his left foot in front of his right, gave it more of his weight, and waited to hear something. When nothing happened, he carefully put his right foot in front of his left, feeling like one of those circus performers walking on a tightrope.

"Don't mess around up there. Just shake the branch free," Nick called up.

Nick's impatient voice made Trino mad. What did he expect? Trino, the squirrel? Running across the branches like nothing? Why didn't Nick get up here and see how fast he moved?

Another crack. Trino heard it loud and clear. And then he knew, slow and careful wasn't going to do the job. Quickly, Trino gauged the distance of his body from the tips of the branches he needed to shake loose. Three steps, probably, and he could kick the branch free.

He glanced up, decided what his hands would do at the same time he got his feet moving, and then took a deep breath.

He ignored the cracks, three of them, as his feet stepped down the branch. He gripped both hands above him, scraping them as they moved down the branch above his head, but he was determined not to let go, no matter what. He raised his leg and shoved his foot into the tangle of branches.

The whole tree seemed to shiver and shake, and as he gripped tighter, he kicked harder. Sticks cracked, dry leaves rustled, and with a *whooshing* sound, the branch fell towards the ground. As soon as he saw the branch dropping, taking two other branches with it, Trino stepped backwards quickly. His hands followed the fast pace to get him away from the sounds of falling branches. Suddenly, his feet felt empty. Instead of moving backwards, they were going down, down. Sounds of breaking tree limbs mingled with Trino's strangling yell. He felt a jerking in his arms, but kept the tightest grip he had ever held locked firmly around the branch above him. Somehow, he thought to start swinging his legs, and found something to touch with his feet.

He heard Nick calling his name, but Trino was too busy to answer. He glanced down only a second to see that the branch where he had been standing had broken off, but only halfway. He forced his hands to slide backwards on the limb above him until he got his feet back on the jagged branch. First his toes, then his feet, and finally, wobbly, shaking legs came to rest on that piece of tree.

Trino got his hands even with his body, then he was upright, steady. He moved as quickly as he could until he could hug the trunk. It wasn't until that moment when he allowed himself to breathe normally.

"Trino? Are you okay? Trino!"

"I'm . . . I'm oh . . . okay." Trino spoke between welcome breaths. He was so glad to be breathing at all.

"Well, get down here before you break your neck," Nick yelled up.

"No kidding!" Trino's voice was thick with sarcasm. And the anger his words carried gave him strength to get down the tree carefully, but quickly.

Nick was already dragging other branches towards the rusty red pick-up he used for tree jobs. Trino grabbed hold of the branch that nearly got him killed and took a lot of pleasure in dragging it over the rocks in the driveway.

They worked together silently until all the branches were loaded. Then Trino got the canvas cover out of the truck cab and helped Nick spread it over the branches and tie it down.

"Okay. Let me get our money, and we'll head to the dump. Wait here," Nick said, swiping his arm across his sweaty face.

Trino just nodded and opened the door of the truck. Leaving the door open, he sat on the bench seat, and leaned over towards the jug of water Nick carried. He lifted it too easily and knew it was empty. "Aw, man," he muttered, his thoat and mouth feeling like he had eaten sawdust for lunch. He tossed the jug aside and turned to stare at the side of the house.

His black eyes glided over the windows, but he could not see anything inside. It was a nice enough house, with clean-looking brick walls and dark trim. The back yard had a garden, a cement patio, trimmed grass and flowers. Just from looking at the neat appearance, Trino had decided the owner had no children. Nothing looked like it had been walked upon, and the yard wasn't junked up with broken toys.

It was then that Trino spied the water faucet towards the front of the house. He grabbed the water jug, got out of the truck, and walked towards it quickly. The water that rushed from the faucet was cool and wet as Trino let it run over his fingers and hands. He propped the jug with his leg to fill it up as he wiped his wet hands over his face and neck. As the jug reached halfway, he raised it to his mouth and drank in big gulps.

He was refilling it again when he heard angry voices on the front porch. Afraid the owner might get mad for using his water, Trino quickly shut off the faucet. He was just putting the jug back into the front seat when he spied Nick coming around the house. His tall body was slightly bent at the waist, as if he were ready to grab something — or someone — and break it into two pieces with his big hands. His dark face looked mean and angry, with tiny black slits instead of eyes. His lips seemed to disappear completely.

Trino swallowed hard as he got into the truck, slamming the door shut. Whatever was wrong with Nick, well . . . Trino just wanted to stay out of his way.

Nick jerked open the door of the driver's side and slid under the steering wheel. He cursed in Spanish as he started the truck.

"What's wrong?" Trino asked automatically, then regretted saying anything when Nick ground the gears loudly as he shifted and drove the truck forward.

This morning Nick had backed up the truck into the driveway of the house so they could load the branches easily. Now they were headed towards the street, only Nick didn't drive that far. He stopped when the back of the truck was parallel to the front porch, a wooden framed area that had a nice wooden glider, flower pots, and an expensive-looking front door.

As Nick got out of the truck, a man came out of the house. Trino assumed it was the man who had hired Nick to trim the tree in the back corner of his yard. He looked like a pit-bull, with pointed features and small ears against his balding head. His clothes were new-looking, his white shirt clean, and his brown shorts fitted around his stout legs.

"Hey! What are you doing?" the man yelled out to Nick.

"We agreed upon a price. If you're not going to pay me what you said you would, then you can have your damn tree back. Trino! Come help unload this man's tree."

Trino jumped when Nick yelled for him and got out of the truck as fast as he could.

"Are you crazy?" the man yelled.

Trino wondered the same thing. Only who was the crazy one?

Nick had already untied the ropes. He pulled a thick branch from under the canvas, then turned around with the branch in his hand as if he were going to use it as a weapon. He walked towards the man on the porch, squeezing his hand around the branch so hard that chunks of bark fell onto the clean sidewalk.

Trino's heart pounded as he saw Nick raise the branch as if he were going to strike the man. The man's eyes were wide, but Trino could not tell if he was scared. Trino was worried.

He had no doubt that Nick was strong enough to kill someone. Over tree money?

Suddenly, Nick tossed the branch down on the porch, just barely missing the man's brown leather shoes. Nick turned and headed towards the truck.

"Get every branch, Trino. We don't want to *cheat* Mr. Caballero out of his tree. Get every leaf and every little stick out of our truck. Give 'em back to Mr. Caballero."

Trino lifted the canvas up as Nick grabbed another branch, this one with scratchy leaves attached to it. This, too, he threw on the porch. Then Nick pulled three logs down on the sidewalk despite the man's cursing at him.

As Trino untangled a longer branch and pulled it out of the pile, he noticed the dried-up bees' nest that had crumbled between the branches and loudly said, "Nick, do we give him back the branches with the bees' nests, too?"

"Hell, yes, give him back his bees! I got stung twice today. I should've gotten extra pay just in case I go to the clinic tonight," Nick said. He ripped apart branches as he tried to untangle them.

Trino grabbed hold of a small branch that still had some of the bees' nest clinging to it.

He pulled it out and turned himself so that the man on the porch could see it. "I read about these bees in science class, Nick. This is the nest of those killer bees."

"Hey! Wait! Stop! Stop! Put that branch back into the truck, boy! You can have your money. Just get these branches off my property. Now!" The man's brown face was almost the color of his brick house as he yelled at them.

Very calmly, Nick shoved the branch back under the canvas. He surveyed all the branches around him and said. "Now I got to clean up around here, too. Two hundred dollars, Mr. Caballero." He motioned at Trino to put his branch away, too.

Mr. Caballero grumbled some curse words in Spanish as he opened his wallet and pulled out some bills. He thrust them towards Nick, who merely pulled them from his fingers.

The man kicked at the branch closest to him. "Now clean up this mess before my wife gets home." Then he went inside the house, slamming the door behind him.

Nick looked at Trino and raised one eyebrow. "He was supposed to give me one-fifty for the job." Before Trino could say anything about taking his share, Nick said, "Hurry up! Let's go, before Caballero changes his mind again."

Quickly, Trino ran to the porch and picked up the branch. It was much heavier than he expected—only reaffirming how physically strong Nick was.

"So what are you going to do with the extra fifty dollars?" Trino had waited until they had left Mr. Caballero's neighborhood before asking.

From his spot behind the steering wheel, Nick gave Trino a quick look. "Keep it in my wallet. Why?"

Trino felt cheated. "I'm the one who scared Mr. Caballero about the bees. That was my idea."

"I see," Nick said. "So if you had an extra fifty bucks, what would you do with it?"

Trino started to open his mouth, but instead turned to look out the truck window. He let his elbow rest on the open window as he felt the hot wind brush against his face. *Fifty bucks? It might as well be five hundred or five million like the lottery jackpot – none of it was his – even a stinking fifty dollars.*

"What does it matter?" Trino said out loud.

"I got plans for the money," Nick replied. "If I thought you had a plan, maybe I'd share it with you."

"Screw you, man." Trino turned to give Nick a burning glare. "You wouldn't share it. Even if I told you I was saving up to buy a car. I work just as hard as you do. But I don't get anything but a lousy twenty bucks."

"You think I'm cheating you, huh, boy?" Nick's voice got louder, but his face didn't look as angry as Trino had seen it other times. "Well, I'll tell you what; if you can go out and find a tree job for the two of us to do, I'll take the twenty bucks and you can have the rest. You settle up whatever price you want with the owner — and you got to pay for gas in the truck — but I'll do your job if you can do mine."

Suddenly Trino's throat felt very dry, but Nick's challenge only made Trino want to succeed. He had to show Nick that Trino Olivares was worth more than twenty bucks.

Remembering that Nick always sealed their bargains with his handshake, Trino extended his hand. "You got a deal, Nick. *I'm* going to find us a tree job."

The older man reached over and clasped Trino's sweating hand. "Let's just see what you can do, boss man."

Trino's fingers had gripped Nick's hand when he caught a glimpse of brown out of the corner of his eye. In a split second, he turned his head and yelled, "Nick! Watch out!"

Chapter Two
Sticks and Stones

The deer had bounded onto the highway with a sudden leap, landing only inches from the front end of Nick's truck. Its brownish-gray fur had blended into the road, but Trino had seen the rack of antlers and the jerk of its head.

Nick's reflexes were good, but just not fast enough to avoid crashing into the deer. Its body flipped up and slid over the hood of the truck, coming fast at Trino's side of the front windshield. It slammed against the window, then fell off the side of the truck.

Trino couldn't catch his breath. Nick wrestled with the steering wheel. He had yelled out when the deer hit the windshield.

The truck spun in a circle, off the highway road into the dirt ditch. Trino pushed his hands against the dashboard, trying to keep his butt on the seat. Dust and dirt filled his mouth and eyes. His head bumped the ceiling, then he fell against Nick, and was tossed again back towards his door. His heart seemed to stop beating inside him.

The confusion lasted only seconds, but once the truck finally stopped and Trino could hear his own breathing, he wondered if it was still the same day as it was before.

It took a moment for Trino's head to start working again. Dirt stung his eyes, but he tried to see where they were.

Nick had managed to stop the truck before it hit a wire fence. But it was a close call because Trino's side of the truck was so tight against the fence, he couldn't even open his door and get out.

"You okay, Trino?" Nick asked for the second time that day.

He managed to cough out something that sounded like, "Yeah. I'm okay."

Then he thought to look at the older man and say, "Are you okay, Nick?"

Nick's face was a mess of sweat and dirt, his eyes red and wide. He dropped his hands from the steering wheel and relaxed his back into the truck seat. "Well . . . yeah. I don't feel any broken bones, but I got a headache from hitting the door a couple of times."

"Me, too." Trino rubbed the top of his head, then groaned when his fingers hit a sore spot.

"Stupid deer."

Nick straightened up to look in the rearview mirror. "I wonder if we can find it. Man, we could have a good venison barbeque tonight."

"What?" Trino couldn't believe what Nick had said. His truck was off the road, both of them had eaten dirt, got banged around inside the truck, and he wanted to go find some dead deer to eat for supper?

"You've never eaten deer meat? If you cook it over a pit—this old man showed me how to season it with garlic and onion, add a few tomatoes and — it gets so tender. Just lay it onto some warm tortillas and you got some tacos that are *muy ricos*."

Trino didn't know whether to feel hungry or to worry that Nick's bump on the head had made him crazy, especially when Nick started laughing.

"Did we go on a wild ride or what? You know people pay money at the carnival for a ride like we just had. Do you realize we spun in a circle? Man!"

Now that it was over, Trino had to admit that if he hadn't been so scared, it could have been fun. At least when he rode a carnival ride like the Zoomer, he wasn't eating dirt or worried that a deer was going to come through the windshield and hit him in the face. Later, all this would make a good story to tell, but right now Trino just wanted to get home and get away from Nick for awhile.

It took some time, but Nick maneuvered the truck out of the ditch without anyone having to get out and push. Trino was glad for that. But he thought Nick didn't need to go back down the road a mile looking for a dead deer. He was relieved when Nick finally said, "I just don't see it. Too bad," and turned the truck back in the direction of the town dump.

Both of them were quiet for the rest of the drive. They unloaded the branches where a man wearing a red baseball cap told them to go, and then, after what seemed like hours and hours of sweaty work without any food, Nick drove them back to the trailer park where Trino lived with his mother and three younger brothers.

A group of young boys was kicking around a soccer ball in the gravel parking lot between house trailers. Trino's little brothers, Gus and Beto, came running from the group as soon as they saw Nick's truck.

"Hey, Nick," Beto said, wheezing as he talked. "Did you bring us something?"

Gus just made a running jump for Nick's legs and grabbed onto him. "Nick! Nick!"

"Hi, boys. Where's your mom?" Nick said, swinging Gus by the arms as he walked away from the truck.

"Do you got treats?" Beto asked Nick, reaching up to grab his hand.

"No, no treats today, boys." Nick looked over at Trino and raised a black eyebrow. "Just two tired men who worked hard all day."

"Awwww!" Both little boys groaned out their disappointment.

Trino couldn't blame them. In the past few weeks that Nick had hung around, he had often brought a variety of good things to eat, like brown bags of barbeque sausage, a sack of oranges or apples, or a pizza or two. He usually had a few candies in his pockets for Gus and Beto.

Not today. Trino didn't look forward to going inside their family's trailer. His mom would probably fix egg tacos. Since she had lost her job two weeks ago, it seemed as if the only thing they ate was eggs. Trino started to wonder if he'd grow feathers soon.

Beto and Gus led the way inside, followed by Trino, then Nick. Trino's mom sat on the faded brown sofa, sorting socks and underwear from a plastic clothes basket and piling them around her. "You boys go wash your hands! And don't you touch these clean clothes or you'll get it, you hear me? Trino, did you get your pay yet? Go to Epifaño's and buy some milk . . . oh! Buy some eggs. We only have four left, and Nick needs to eat, too."

Trino didn't want to go to the store. He was tired. He glanced around looking for Félix, wondering where his lazy brother was hiding.

"I don't have any money," Trino stated.

"You don't have money? Well, where's your pay? Didn't you work?" His mom's voice rose in volume as she rose from the sofa. She pushed her black hair out of her face and gave Nick a mean look. "You're both dirty enough. Didn't my boy earn something today? You know how tight things are around here, Nick."

"He's got twenty dollars comin'," Nick said in a slow voice. "I got it in my pocket."

"Well, let me have it, and I'll give a little to Trino to go to the store."

"Mom, I'm tired. Why can't Félix go to the store?"

Trino felt mad at everybody. He was getting nothing out of sweating today and nearly getting killed — twice! Now he had to walk to the store and come home to eat egg tacos, or egg sandwiches, or eggs and beans — and that was the worst because everybody got smelly gas afterwards. What a lousy day!

"Nick, can I have Trino's pay?" His mom held out her hand to Nick.

The tall man looked down at her hand, then looked at Trino. He reached into the pocket of his dirt-streaked workshirt and pulled out a twenty-dollar bill.

Trino's mother made a quick motion to snatch the money from Nick's dark fingers, but Nick flipped the bill back into his fist. He looked steadily at her.

"No, María. This is Trino's money. He did a man's job today. And he should have some say about what he does with his paycheck."

"Don't be stupid, Nick. The boy's earning some money so we can eat. You think somebody asks me what I want to do with my paycheck? I give everything to keep this family going. Trino's old enough to start helping this family, too."

"I have no problem with Trino working to help his family. But you don't have to take away every quarter so he can't even buy himself or his brothers a piece of candy."

Neither Gus nor Beto had said anything until they heard the word "candy." They started to jump up and down, bouncing against their mother.

"I want some candy!" Beto exclaimed. "I want some candy!"

"Candy! Candy!" Gus echoed. "Candy? Candy?"

Her response was to grab each boy by the arm and start dragging them towards the bathroom. "Stop it! I'm not going to listen to you two cry for candy. Trino, go to the store like I told you. Nick, you can wash up at the sink."

Trino waited until his mom had left the living room before he turned to look at Nick. The man's lips were pressed together, as if he didn't want to talk. He just handed Trino the crumpled twenty-dollar bill.

Shoving it into the front pocket of his jeans, Trino made it a point to slam the screen door behind him.

Why can't I be like Félix and be lazy? I want to be Gus and Beto and play with my friends all day. Why do I have to work, but my mom spends the money? Why doesn't she go find a job? Then I could spend my money my way.

Suddenly, Trino could hear Nick's voice haunting him like a ghost: *"And what would you do with extra money? Do you have a plan?"*

As Trino made his way out of the trailer park, he wondered what kind of plan any thirteen-year-old boy could have. He looked down at his shoes: torn-up, scarred leather sneakers that his mother brought home last summer. What would it be like to wear a pair of shoes that somebody else hadn't worn first?

He walked through the neighborhood, considering cars, television sets that didn't fuzz out all the time, a stereo that could blast music through the house. But who would pay for gas? For cable? For extra CDs? Even though he was hungry, he quickly decided that buying extra hamburgers or pizza wasn't worth it—once he ate it, the food and the money were gone. No, if he had some money, he'd have to think about buying something really good.

His thinking took him towards the busy street where old Epifaño ran his little store.

Trino had only been back once since the robbery a month ago. That day, Trino had seen Rosca and two others beating up Mr. Epifaño, and when they had realized that Trino was watching, they had chased him. For weeks Trino worried that Rosca would kill him, and once Trino had proved he wouldn't squeal, Rosca expected Trino to be on Rosca's side for other things, like breaking into a car wash and stealing the money.

That night at the car wash, Trino had seen his best friend killed and his other friend fall apart from the shock. Two weeks had gone by, and still Trino walked around with a gut full of loneliness for the three of them who had hung around together since they were little kids. Working with Nick had kept him busy. At school, he could fill his mind with teacher junk. Only at lunch time and on Sundays did he miss the guys and think about them.

Trino paused outside the store, relieved to see the front window had finally been replaced.

The last time he had come by, the front had a big board covering the broken glass. It had been broken when Rosca had thrown a pipe at Trino as he had run out of the store.

Slowly, Trino pushed the silver bar on the glass door to let himself into the store. He had the oddest feeling that he just had done everything the same as another time. Trino had been coming to Epifaño's store for years. Maybe that was it.

There were a couple of ladies in the store, a skinny girl holding a baby in her arms, and a man standing by the magazines talking very loud, as if half-deaf or something. Trino made his way back to the refrigerated shelves where Epifaño kept the eggs and milk. It was cooler in that part of the store, and Trino stood there longer. He liked the feel of cold air on his sweaty skin.

That's when he noticed the bags of cookies on a corner shelf. His attention was drawn to the chocolate cookies with the vanilla creme in the middle. Everyone in the family loved those cookies, but no one had eaten any in weeks.

"Too much money," she said, the last time Beto asked their mother why she didn't buy cookies. "I can buy a bag of beans, some bread, and a sack of potatoes for what some cookies cost me."

For the first time in his life, Trino leaned over to look at a price tag. $3.79. It *did* seem like a lot of money for a bag of cookies. He was tempted to buy them anyway, just so he could walk in with something special for them—like Nick did sometimes. Only he wasn't Nick. His mother would get mad if he wasted that much money on cookies.

And then he saw the bag of white marshmallows on a lower shelf. The price tag read 87¢. It seemed like a small enough price for a family treat. He took a bag, then reached back to get the carton of eggs and the plastic milk jug.

Heading towards the front counter, he walked down the aisle of soaps and cleaners. He slowed his pace as he saw that the owner of the store was back at the register. Mr. Epifaño wore a weird brown hat with a narrow brim, and it seemed to be covering a bandage that poked out from behind his ear. Yellow and red bruises still spotted his brown face. A thin scar ran across his forehead down past his nose. One of his arms was wrapped in a blue bandage and rested inside a white sling.

Old Mr. Epifaño half-stepped, half-slid around, as he put things in a bag for the girl with the baby, took her money, and gave her change. He only said a few words, and didn't smile like he usually did.

It hurt Trino to see the old man so banged up. A memory of Epifaño's bloody face suddenly resurfaced. Trino had heard the beating, had seen Rosca with the pipe, hitting the old man.

Trino swallowed hard. He thought, *eggs and milk, eggs and milk; get out of the store with eggs and milk.*

"Hey—boy—you!"

It took Trino a second to realize the old man's grunts were words, directed at him.

Did he remember that Trino was here that day?

Trino felt something hot spinning around in his stomach. He forced his hands to put the marshmallows, egg carton, and milk jug on the counter. He concentrated on his two fingers pulling the twenty-dollar bill out of his jeans pocket.

"What—what's—your—name?"

Trino raised his eyes carefully. He met the old man's gaze only when Trino was sure nothing would betray him. He saw a glassy look in Epifaño's eyes, like tears. Did he remember? Did he know that Trino saw everything that happened to him?

Suddenly, the old man pushed his face closer to Trino's, as if he wanted a better look.

The action startled Trino, so he jumped back a little. He wanted just to keep going out the door, but then he'd look like he was hiding something. He caught himself. He stood up straight, and didn't let his face betray the nervous fear inside him.

"I seen you—before—I know—you." Epifaño's slow words sounded scratchy and hoarse.

Trino shrugged his shoulders. "I've been coming to this store a long time. Sometimes I'm with my mom." He figured if he mentioned his mother, the old man would stop staring so hard. He wanted someone else to come up to the counter, needing to buy something—anything so Epifaño would take Trino's money and let him get out of here.

He pushed the twenty-dollar bill across the counter. "Here's money for the stuff I want."

Epifaño jerked his head up at the same moment that Trino felt a pair of heavy hands clamp down on his shoulders.

"Hey, Tío, why can't we just use this kid?"

Chapter Three
Broken Branches

Trino's body stiffened up. Who had him by the shoulders? And what did he want?

"Hey! What do you want? I didn't do anything. I got money to pay for this food." Trino's voice sounded strong. He was in the right, and he was glad he didn't sound like some scared kid.

"Let him go, Armando." Mr. Epifaño's voice was steady now. The old man had straightened up as he spoke to his nephew. "What's your name, boy?" he asked Trino.

"Why do you want to know?" Trino wriggled out from the nephew's grip and took a step aside. He shot a dirty look at the man who had been holding him. It was the same guy he had seen by the magazines, the one who had been talking too loud.

He felt suspicious of both of these men staring at him, even though neither one looked mad or anything.

"I'm looking for a boy to help me in the store for a few weeks," Mr. Epifaño said.

"I can't sweep, and I need somebody to help with the boxes in the back room. I can't pay but a few dollars, but I'll give you a little food—*para tu familia*. I seen you in here—with your mama or your brothers. I never seen you steal from me, so I guess I could trust you, eh?"

Trino shifted his weight side to side on his feet as his hands slid down into his pockets. Well, he hadn't stolen *that much* from Epifaño—a couple of candy bars here and there. And he *did* put in two of his own quarters *before* he bumped the video machine to give him free games.

Suddenly, a long finger pressed Trino's shoulder. The voice was loud and impatient.

"Well, boy, do you want the job? Can you work for my Tío?"

The poke seemed to clear Trino's head. *A job!*

And he remembered how Nick had acted around people he worked for. Trino extended his hand to Mr. Epifaño. "My name is Trino Olivares. I can work for a few weeks, Mr. Epifaño."

"Can you come tomorrow?" Mr. Epifaño asked him, then turned to the register to ring up Trino's purchase.

Trino thought for a second, remembered what he wanted to do tomorrow, and quickly tried to figure out a way to do both. "I can come in the morning for a couple of hours."

"*Mañana — como a las diez de la mañana.*"

"Okay, I'll be here at ten o'clock." Trino picked up the twenty-dollar bill and gave it to Mr. Epifaño.

"You got your helper, Tío. Now we don't got to worry about you anymore," the nephew said, as he grabbed a candy bar from a box on the counter. He ripped open the wrapper and started eating it as he walked out of the store.

What a jerk. I'm glad he's not in my family, Trino told himself as he took his change and saw the old man fumble with the white plastic bag he wanted to use.

"I can do it, Mr. Epifaño," Trino said, and held it open while the old man placed the eggs and the marshmallows inside. He grabbed the milk jug with the other hand and said, "See you tomorrow at ten."

As Trino left the corner store, he didn't feel tired any-more. He was bringing food home for his family and he had another way to make a little money. This time he'd keep the money for himself—for something good. He wouldn't tell anyone about this job. And he would make a plan for his money. That's what Nick said he needed. And even though he still didn't have a plan by the time he reached the house trailer, Trino still felt like things could be better for him.

"Here are your eggs and milk," Trino told his mother as soon as he saw her in the kitchen. The house already smelled of bacon grease and frying tortillas.

"*Ay*, it's about time," she said, sighing and pushing her black hair out of her face.

Trino quickly pulled the eggs out of the bag and put them on the counter by the stove. He wrapped the bag around his "surprise" for the family and shoved it back behind the cans on top of the refrigerator. "Mr. Epifaño's back at the store," he said.

His mother moved away to crack eggs in a brown bowl by the sink. "How does he look?"

"Not too bad," Trino answered, but in a way he was glad the old man was still banged up.

He had a chance to make a little money for himself now. He pulled dollar bills and coins from his pocket and put it near the sink. "Here's the change, Mom."

He was surprised when his mother grabbed his arm with a cool, wet hand. "Trino—"

They were the same height now, and he could look directly into her black eyes, the same eyes that he saw when he looked in the mirror.

"Yeah?"

Her eyes passed over his face before she whispered, "*Gracias.*" And then she turned back to her work as if the moment had never passed between them. "Go take a shower. You smell dirty."

≈ ≈ ≈

Despite the egg meals they had already eaten the past weeks, this one was better than the others. Maybe it was because Trino had been starving after taking a shower. Maybe it was the fried corn tortillas that had been mixed into the eggs. Or maybe that spicy *salsa* that Nick had ground up in the *molcajete* with peppers, tomatoes, *cilantro*, and onions had made the eggs so delicious.

Whatever, he felt full inside after he ate, especially as he and Nick told his mother about the exciting things that happened to them during the day. Of course, *she* got excited that Trino had almost fallen out of the tree and that they had hit the deer and spun around in the truck, but Nick had a way of telling his stories that still made her laugh. Trino did notice, though, that Nick told about Mr. Caballero trying to cheat them, but he didn't mention getting the extra money. Maybe Nick was afraid that Trino's mom would hold out her hand and ask for that, too.

Usually, after a meal, little Gus and Beto were anxious to leave and go outside with their friends. But Trino had noticed that whenever Nick was eating with them, his little brothers stayed at the table, and often one or both would climb onto Nick's lap. He saw the way they were growing attached to the man, and it bothered Trino. What if Nick left like the other men had? Then Trino would get stuck explaining why Nick didn't come around anymore. It always seemed to work out that way.

But at least for tonight, Trino knew he could be someone special for his brothers, too.

"Hey, guys," he said, standing up from the table. "I got a surprise for us."

"A surprise? Is it a toy?" Beto climbed up on his knees at his chair.

"Sooprize?" Gus, who sat in Nick's lap, looked like he was going to climb onto the table.

Trino walked over to the refrigerator and pulled the bag out from behind the cans. Rather than get his brothers into a fight over who opened the bag, he held it in two hands and presented it to his mother like it was a gift wrapped in special paper.

"What's this?" she asked with a frown.

Trino said nothing, hoping she wouldn't get mad that he had spend the extra 87¢ on a "*sooprize*."

"Marsh—smell—ohs!" Gus called out when his mother pulled the package of marshmallows out of the white bag.

"Mama, can I have some?" Beto's black eyes were wide and shiny. "Can I have two—no, three—three? Three of them?"

Their mother pressed her fingers down on the bag and then looked up at Trino. Her eyebrows were still wrinkled together in a frown.

"I didn't pay much for them, Mom—and Nick usually has a little candy for Gus and Beto—but we were busy today—I thought everybody could share them." His reasons were jumbled together in his head and came out as he thought of them. "Yeah—we could all share—and stuff—like—that—" His voice trailed off when his mother's expression didn't change.

That's when Nick reached over and put his hand on her arm. "Buying the marshmallows was a good thing to do, Trino. Don't you think so, María?"

She looked at Nick then, and Trino noticed the slight movement of Nick's head in Trino's direction. Then he raised one eyebrow and stared at her for a long moment.

Trino's mom released a breath, then nodded slowly. She looked at Trino as she spoke. "It was good to think of your little brothers and buy them something." Her words were slow, as if it was hard to say them at all.

"Hey, I like marshmallows—I mean marsh—smell—ohs—too," Nick said, then laughed and tickled Gus around the waist. "Do you want some of Trino's marsh—smell—ohs, Gus?"

Trino smiled as he saw Gus and Beto laugh with Nick. Even their mother smiled a little as Nick's big hand flipped palm up, and he said in a squeaky, funny voice, "Can we all have some marsh—smell—ohs, Mama—please?" He winked at Trino before his voice returned to normal. "And then we all need to tell Trino, thanks for the marshmallows."

Both little boys managed a "thanks," but it was squishy and white as it came out of their mouths. Trino took three marshmallows, and it appeared that even his mom enjoyed a couple of them before she stood up and started to clear the table.

"I wonder where Félix is. *Ay*, that boy! Trino, go out and see if you can find him at Nacho's house. You tell him I said if he doesn't come home, I'm going to give his supper to Mrs. Peña's cat."

Trino groaned, then went back to find his old sneakers. He pulled them on, not bothering with socks and just left them untied. Nacho didn't live far, and if Félix wasn't there, he was probably at Manolo's or Frank's house. They all lived on the same street.

The evening had cooled down, and it was still light enough to walk around and not worry about tripping over someone's junk or a dumb kid jumping at you from between the cars.

Trino was walking, thinking about what to do with money he'd get from Mr. Epifaño, when a boy stepped from behind a row of trees that acted like a fence between Nacho's house and the street.

"Trino?" The voice shook as it repeated, "Trino?"

Trino stopped to stare, but he could hardly believe who stood in front of him. "Rogelio? Is that you, Rogelio?"

"Rogelio," he repeated, and stepped a little closer.

Now Trino could see confusion in Rogelio's dark eyes. His hair had been shaved really short. His clothes had always been wrinkled, but this time they looked dirty, too. "Rogelio, what happened to you, man? I been to your house a couple of times, but your *abuelita*—your grandmother—she wouldn't tell me nothing. You okay, man?"

"You okay, man," Rogelio said in a dead voice and suddenly Trino got mad.

He grabbed Rogelio by the arms and shook him twice. "Are you stupid?" he said in a loud voice. "Do you just have to repeat everything? Ever since I've known you, all you did was repeat whatever me or Zipper said. Tell me what happened to you after they arrested you at the car wash. What happened to Rosca? Do you know?"

Rogelio just stared at Trino, but he did start talking. His breath smelled like rotten eggs.

"They took me downtown, man. But I didn't have a record, so my dad came the next day and got me out. Later I got it bad with his belt. Now I gotta see a Juve officer once a week. And I go to this school run by priests. It sucks, man. Look at my hair. I wear a uniform, too—might as well be in prison."

Trino shook his head. "Naw, man, you don't want to go there." He still remembered what that poet Montoya had written about his prison days. Not to have any freedom or privacy, to get kicked around by other prisoners and the guards—no, it wasn't what he wanted for Rogelio—but maybe there were others who deserved it. "And what about Rosca, man? Do know what happened to him?"

By now, Trino had released Rogelio. His old friend nodded in answer to the question.

"Yeah, I heard about Rosca. He's gone to some prison boot camp until his trial comes up. My Juve officer said the police had him fingered for a couple of other robberies, and he beat up old Epifaño, too. Did you know that?"

Sure I know. Trino merely shrugged his shoulders. "Rosca was always mean."

"Been—been—" Rogelio looked around him, as if was afraid someone else was there.

"Been wondering about you, too—and thinking about—" his voice lowered as he said, "Zipper."

The incident came back to Trino like he was living it again. Trino had stopped by a car wash stall, trying to catch his breath. He had run from his house, late for his meeting with Rogelio, Zipper, Rosca, and the others. Trino had seen Rogelio, Zipper, and Rosca banging on the towel machines with crowbars, trying to get money from them. Suddenly, the old man in the red shirt had come out from behind the dumpster. He had a gun in his hand. Yelling, running for the man, Rosca had raised his crowbar. There was a gunshot and Rosca fell. Zipper yelled out and started running towards Rosca. Zipper spooked the old man, who shot at him, too. Rosca was wounded, but Zipper was dead. Poor Rogelio had been left there, crying and repeating Zipper's last words, "No, no, no."

What had happened two weeks ago, that night at the car wash, when he saw his friend get killed, would stay with Trino all his life. He was learning to live with that awful memory, like a red, wrinkled scar from a bad burn. But as he looked at Rogelio, he wondered if there was still any friendship left between them.

"Hey, Rogelio, why don't you and I do something tomorrow?" he suggested, not ready to give up now that he had finally made contact.

"No, no," Rogelio said, shaking his head. "No, no. I got to stay away from you. You're just trouble. No, no." He spoke like he was repeating what someone else had told him. He sounded like a robot and a scared one at that.

Suddenly, they heard a loud whistle, then another.

Rogelio shook his head with jerky movements from side to side. He backed away, towards the trees. Then before Trino could say anything, Rogelio bolted, running down the street as if a pack of dogs was after him.

That's when Trino heard boys' laughter, and his brother Félix's voice, "Aw, man, can't you whistle any better than that?"

The whistle sounded again as Trino stepped around the trees and saw Félix, his friends Nacho and Frank, sitting on the porch of Nacho's house. Each of them took turns pinching his lips and making loud whistle sounds, trying to outwhistle the one before.

"Félix!" Trino felt dumb that he was still looking over his shoulder for Rosca and let his frustration out on his brother. "Where you been? You need to get your butt home now, before I climb up on that porch and kick it home!"

Félix responded by signaling a "wait" with his hands, then let one more whistle go. It sounded so much like the one Rosca used to make.

"Where did you learn to make that sound?" Trino asked Félix as they walked home.

"No place," Félix answered, and just stuck his hands into his jeans pockets.

"Did you see Rogelio? I was talking to him just before I called you."

"We saw him. Nacho said he's all messed up ever since he saw Zipper get wasted."

Trino shoved his brother so hard, Félix fell off the curb into the street. His brother started cussing at him, but Trino didn't care. He just kept walking back towards the trailer park.

He was so mad at Rogelio and even Zipper for being so stupid. He had never let himself feel anger at them for following Rosca like a pair of hungry dogs after a bone. *We were all stupid,* he told himself, *but I guess I'm the only one left to admit it.*

And then he turned as he heard the running footsteps behind him. Trino didn't even try to stop his brother when Félix shoved him roughly. Trino caught his balance before he fell, and almost laughed at the sight of his brother's back as he quickly ran all the way back to the trailer.

"You're lucky I'm tired out from working. Or I'd whip your butt good!" Trino called out to his little brother.

He walked home alone, feeling like a dangling branch that finally broke off a tree. He had no choice but to find something else for himself. Except that he had no idea where to look.

Chapter Four

Yardstick

"What's all this?" Mr. Epifaño's voice was louder than Trino had ever heard it before.

Trino quickly tossed aside the car magazine he had found behind some boxes. He felt stupid for getting caught when he had only stopped working a couple of minutes ago to flip through the magazine.

"What?" He looked at the old man and shrugged, trying to hide his embarrassment. "I cleaned up the room — just like you told me."

"You call this clean?" Mr. Epifaño pointed with the hand that wasn't trapped in a sling.

"I told you to put stuff away. *Mira* — look here." He limped over to the boxes that Trino had shoved in the corner. "Some of these boxes are empty. Why didn't you throw them outside in the dumpster?"

Trino shrugged again. "You didn't tell me that I could throw stuff away."

"And I thought you were going to sweep the floor," the man said, pointing towards the warped gray tiles that he and Trino stood upon.

"I swept up." Trino looked down. The floor in the storeroom was so old, how could anyone tell if it was clean or dirty?

Using one foot, Mr. Epifaño moved a box aside. He slid it closer to the wall. A thin, long mound of dirt was left behind. It outlined the space where Trino had just swept dirt to the edges and left the middle space cleaner.

"You want me to pay you, you got to do things right, boy. And you got to use your *cabeza*. I shouldn't have to say 'throw this away,' or move the boxes as you sweep up the room. *¿Entiendes?*"

"Yeah—okay," Trino mumbled, knowing he was going to have to start the job all over.

He wondered what time it was. He wanted to get out of here before twelve.

Mr. Epifaño slowly turned around. "Yeah, empty boxes toss out—oh! And the dirt on the floor? You can throw that away, too. Nobody wants to buy my dirt, you know?"

Trino noticed the old man's grin. "I'm not that stupid, Mr. Epifaño." He hated it when someone thought he was dumb. He glared at Mr. Epifaño's face, wishing to burn a hole in it.

Only Mr. Epifaño didn't care. He shuffled out of the storeroom making noises that sounded like laughter.

Trino cussed out his anger about working harder as he started to shove boxes around and pile up the ones that could be tossed in the dumpster. He ran into the magazine again, and thought he should steal it—the cover was ripped up and the date on the front was a year old. But he had no jacket or baggy shirt to hide it while he walked out of the store. Trino just hid it on top of a shelf, in case he worked here another day.

He swept again and stacked the filled boxes in rows against the wall. After he carried the empty boxes outside, he used his *cabeza* to see that he needed to flatten the boxes so they'd fit in the dumpster. Trino went back into the store to see the lighted clock that hung on the wall behind the cash register. *Eleven-fifteen.*

He heard the door to the store open and glanced behind him. It was his brother, Félix, coming inside. Trino quickly ran back into the storeroom, hoping Mr. Epifaño wouldn't make a connection between the boys. No one in the family knew that Trino had taken this job. He wanted this money for himself. This morning he had told his mother that yesterday he had run into Rogelio—which wasn't a lie—and they were going to help Rogelio's grandmother clean up and move some furniture around. Not a "big" lie since he *was* cleaning and moving stuff around.

Trino walked behind the boxes and waited. He listened for the sounds of the video game machines, but didn't hear anything. Maybe Félix came in to buy a candy bar or something. It seemed like Trino waited a long time before he peeked into the store, looking for his brother. Félix was gone, and Trino sighed in relief.

"I'm finished, Mr. Epifaño," he said, coming out of the storeroom. "When do you want me to come again?"

The store owner was straightening the magazines in front of the counter. "I need to put new stuff on the shelves. Can you stay longer?"

Trino shook his head. His mother expected him to be home by noon. Anyway, he wasn't going to give up a whole Sunday until he knew he'd make some decent money. At least with his job with Nick, he knew he'd get twenty dollars. Mr. Epifaño still hadn't given him anything, yet Trino didn't want to make the guy mad at him and get nothing. "I got some things I have to do today for my mom, but I could come back tomorrow after school."

"*Mañana, ¿eh?*" The old man seemed to be chewing over Trino's idea as he pursed his lips together and rubbed his chin. Finally, he nodded, then moved away to straighten up the candy boxes on a nearby shelf.

Trino stood still, watching the man. He waited for Mr. Epifaño to say something about paying him for today's work. He hadn't realized how long he stood in the same spot until a customer behind him said, "Get out of the way, kid, so I can pay for my stuff."

He jumped a little, then stepped closer to the magazine rack, so a fat man could waddle closer. Mr. Epifaño came back around the counter, saying nothing to Trino when he passed him. He rang up the man's cokes and chips, got paid, then shut the cash register again.

Still Trino waited for Mr. Epifaño to talk to him. Instead, the old man sized him up.

"*¡Qué!*" The old man spit out the word.

Trino wanted *something* for cleaning up. Finally, he decided just to hold out his hand and say, "Do I get some money for my work today?"

The old man rubbed his runny nose, wiped his hand on his pants, and finally punched a couple of buttons on the cash register. "Will you come back?"

"I said I would." Trino glanced at the clock. It was almost twelve, and he was getting annoyed by the old man. Why did he move so slow?

Finally, Mr. Epifaño held out two faded bills to Trino. They looked so old, Trino wondered if the bills had been Mr. Epifaño's money when he was a boy. But it was still cash, so Trino took it.

"*Manaña,*" Trino said, then shoved the old dollars into his pocket as he walked out the front door of the store. "Two bucks," he muttered to himself and sighed. But at least it was all his money, not something he had to give to his mom.

As he walked down the sidewalk, he noticed the two boys walking toward him. His black eyebrows raised a little as he recognized them. He wondered if they would even speak to him.

One of the boys was named Jimmy, a tall, slim kid who had been friendly whenever his sister, Lisana, stopped to talk to Trino. From the first time they had met, Trino had noticed that Jimmy walked with his head up and back straight. It wasn't like he was trying to look mean or pretending to be cool. Lisana had that same way about her, only one of many reasons why Trino liked to be around her.

The other boy was called Hector, and he was in Trino's history class third period. After Trino had met Lisana and her friends, Hector had tried to talk to him in class, but Zipper had run him off. He hadn't talked to either boy since Zipper had gotten killed. Only Lisana knew the true story about what happened that night, and he had spoken three times to her at school since then.

Because of Lisana, Trino decided to say, "Hey, how's it going?" He looked into the boys' faces, hoping they might stop and talk a while.

They both looked him over with their dark eyes. Jimmy said, "Hey, man," and Hector shrugged his thick shoulders together. But they just kept walking, both of them stepping out of Trino's path.

Their brush-off made Trino mad.

Screw 'em, he thought, and just kept walking towards home.

~ ~ ~

In the six weeks since Nick had become a regular visitor at their house trailer, Trino had never heard his mom yell at Nick. She'd give him her dirty look or she'd argue about something he wanted to do that cost money she didn't have. As Trino reached the trailer today, he heard his mother's voice, and she sounded plenty mad. And she was using Nick's name a lot as she yelled.

"Nick, what's the matter with you? You think I'm not trying to find a job, Nick? I go out every day and look for work. I got some hungry boys to feed, Nick."

Trino's gut feeling was not to walk inside, but his mother saw him through the screen door.

"Trino! Get inside here. Where have you been all morning?"

Once inside the cramped trailer, he realized why his mother was yelling. Gus and Beto had the TV going full blast. Nick knelt behind the TV. He had pushed it away from the wall, so Beto and Gus were almost sitting under the kitchen table in order to watch it from the odd angle.

"I was out moving stuff—I told you about Rogelio's *abuela*, remember?" Trino found himself yelling in order to hear himself over the TV. He turned towards Nick and said, "Does the TV have to be so loud?"

Suddenly, the TV went dark and the room got quiet.

"Hey!" both boys groaned together.

"Well, I guess that was the wrong knob to turn," Nick said, and frowned at the backside of the television. He scratched his head and sighed.

"We can't watch TV?" Beto asked, his little brown face looking sad and disappointed.

"Maybe later. You *niños* go outside and play now," Nick said, and stood up. He clapped his hands. "Come on! You heard me! Go outside and play." His voice sounded like he was mad, too. Trino wondered if he should follow his brothers out the door. He didn't want to get in the middle of whatever fight his mom and Nick were having.

"Did you have to break our TV, Nick?"

"I didn't break your TV. It was already broken. What good is a TV that's so fuzzy everyone looks like they're covered in cotton balls? I still think there's a loose wire. I'll find it. Then I need to fix that knob for the volume. Your boys are going to go deaf, María." He crossed his arms and fixed his gaze upon her. "And you're changing the subject. We were talking about that job at the college."

Trino's eyebrows raised. His mother working at a college?

"What's he talking about, Mom?" he asked her.

His mother just shook her head and turned her back on Nick and Trino. She walked to the stove and started wiping it down with a rag.

Trino looked at Nick, but the man just ignored Trino and followed Trino's mom into the kitchen area.

"María, you're crazy not to apply for the job."

"I couldn't work in a place like that. Me, I only got to the tenth grade. How could I be around those smart people?"

"Even smart people need someone to clean up their rooms, María."

"Leave me alone, Nick. I don't want to work at the college. I'd feel too stupid around people like that. I can find my own job." His mother's voice got louder. "I don't need you coming in here telling me to get a job and—and—breaking our TV! Why don't you just go home?"

"Be that way!" Nick's voice got loud too. "I got myself out of dead-end jobs. I just wanted to help you do the same thing." He seemed to catch his breath, then his voice grew more even, but he still had more to say. "I really like my job in the Physical Plant. I know Housekeeping could use you, María. I could help you get on there—"

"I don't need your help. I don't need nothing from you." She turned from the stove and threw the rag at Nick. It plopped against Nick's chest, leaving a damp spot on his blue shirt. Nick caught the rag before it fell on the floor. He tossed it on the stove, and just turned to walk out the door. He let the screen door slam behind him.

For the first time, Trino felt sorry for Nick. It seemed like he was trying to help, but his mom was being mean to him. Why was she acting like that?

Trino decided it was better not to ask. If she was mad enough to throw the rag at Nick, she might be mad enough to hit Trino if he said anything she didn't like. Even though he felt hungry, Trino followed Nick's example and walked out of the trailer.

He watched Nick's red truck rumble out of the parking lot and couldn't help but wonder if Nick would ever come back.

≈ ≈ ≈

Usually when Trino's mom was mad, she'd yell and hit them for any reason. And after Nick had gone, Trino decided if she started picking on them, he'd take his little brothers over to the park to get away from her. Only Trino's mom didn't act mean after her fight with Nick. Her face just looked sad. She said nothing as she spread peanut butter on bread slices and poured four glasses of milk. Even when Félix sloshed milk down his T-shirt, she just tossed him a dish towel and walked back to the bedroom. She didn't come out until her *comadre* Irene showed up about an hour later. By then, Gus had fallen asleep on the sofa and Beto was bugging Félix to take him some place. Trino had been fiddling with the TV, trying to fix it, and getting frustrated because he couldn't.

Irene's visits were always an occasion. She worked at a candy factory and usually had a bag of damaged candy boxes for them. She was a fat young woman, leading Trino or Félix always to remark that she must eat more of the candy than she packaged.

She only knocked on the screen door once, before she came into the trailer. Her neon pink T-shirt was pulled tight over the wide hips bulging out of her blue jeans. She swung a faded canvas bag in one hand and carried a black backpack purse in the other.

"Tía Reenie!" Beto called out and started dancing around her. "Tía Reenie, did you bring us candy?"

"No *dulcecitos* 'til I get my *besitos*." She tapped one of her fat brown cheeks, and leaned closer for Beto to kiss her. "*¿Besitos? Ay*, that was a sweet *besito*." Suddenly, she grabbed poor skinny Beto and pressed him against her big breasts. "There's nobody that kisses like my Betito. I just won't get married until Betito can be my husband."

Then she let Beto go and turned her eyes to Trino and Félix, standing by the TV. "I only give candies to the god-sons who kiss me."

Félix and Trino exchanged a pair of worried looks. Neither one of them liked to hug Irene because she crushed you. Her short black hair was itchy. She also smelled like cigarettes and coconut candy. It was a nauseating combination that made you suck air for at least ten minutes.

Luckily, Trino's mom came out of the bedroom, and Tía Reenie decided to hug her instead. "*Ay, comadre*, aren't you eating anything? You're as skinny as my clothesline pole."

Trino's mom gave a little smile to her friend, the woman who was godmother to all of her sons. "How are you, Irene? It's been weeks since you've come by. *¿Por qué?*"

"Well, overtime, that's why. You know how it is, *comadre.* If the boss says he can give you a little extra, you take it, no?" She clapped her hands loudly as she saw Beto climbing on a chair to reach the canvas bag she had left on top of the table among the dirty milk glasses, smears of peanut butter and crumbs. "Hey, boy, don't you be taking anything from the bag until I tell you to."

"I gave you a kiss. I want my candy," Beto told her, his black eyes giving her a serious stare.

This visit Irene had brought more than candy. She had a baseball cap for Félix and a extra-huge green T-shirt for Trino. "My ex-boyfriend left them behind—that two-timing dog. But here—you can wear them." There was a half-filled bottle of bubbles for Gus, who woke up from his nap. She had brought a hair brush for their mom. There were blonde strands tangled in its bristles. "This is how I knew the liar was cheating on me. Do I look like a blonde? Take it, *comadre.* You've got pretty hair. Mine! There's no hope for it. It's a miracle the birds don't nest there." Beto got a bag of odd-sized colored chalk pieces. "Now you can have fun, *mijo,* and don't worry if the colors break. That's the trouble with new things. You're afraid to mess them up. But my presents are broken in—ready to use."

"Trino, take Gus outside with the bubbles, so they don't spill inside. And be sure that Beto doesn't use the chalk on stuff that won't wash off. Go on! All of you outside, so I can visit with Irene in peace," their mother said. She looked tired, but her voice was firm.

"But what about our candy?" Beto asked, only to have his mother push his hand away and pull him down from the table.

"Come on, let's go outside. We can eat candy later." Trino held the bag of broken chalk in one hand and grabbed Beto's arm with the other. The little boy whimpered like a sad puppy. Gus followed them out the door clutching his red bottle of bubbles in his little hands.

As soon as they were outside, Félix put on his "new" cap and said, "I'm going to Nacho's. Later."

Trino put the bag of chalk down on a strip of cement that had once been a curb. "Here, Beto. This is a good place to draw stuff."

"Bubbles! Do bubbles, Trino," Gus said, twisting his fingers around the lid, but not able to open the bottle.

The cap was stuck, but Trino finally got it open. The bottle was half-empty, but at least the plastic wand wasn't broken. He handed the bottle to Gus, then wandered towards the shade of the tree near the back of the house trailer. Gus spilled more bubble juice on himself than he ever blew out. Beto had chalk smeared on his arms, his face, even in the black hair that hung down his forehead. Not thinking much about anything, Trino pressed his back against the tree. His eyes passed over the small open window of his mother's bedroom as he heard women's voices.

"*Comadre*, he told you about a job and you sent him away? Are you crazy?"

"How can I go over there for a job? I didn't even finish high school. And I'm sure the application form is filled with college words I can't even read. And my writing is so awful. Even Beto's first-grade printing is better than mine."

"But, María, you can do the hard cleaning jobs. You're young and strong, even if you are on the skinny side. Look at me, *comadre*. All I'm good for is sitting on my butt and wrapping candies. Anyway, you need to get something better 'cause you got to feed four kids."

"Irene, I just can't go over to there. What would I wear to talk to a man about a job? I haven't bought anything for me in years. I worked in uniforms, and I got by with clothes my sisters didn't want."

"*Comadre*, I got a few good dresses. Maybe one would fit you."

Trino knew it would take three of his mother to fit into one of Tía Reenie's dresses. He sighed as he reached into his pocket and pulled out his two dollars. He stared at the old bills, wishing he could plant them and grow a money tree right in his own back yard.

Chapter Five
Partners

"Not bad, Trino. Always makes me wonder what grades you'd get if you'd actually read the chapter."

Coach Treviño laid a paper on Trino's desk. An 85 was circled in red at the top of the test paper.

Trino shrugged his shoulders, and kept silent about Coach's comment. He always said the same thing whenever Trino got a passing grade. It was pretty easy in this history class because Coach Treviño always told extra stories about the events or the people in a particular chapter. Trino didn't mind listening to him, and usually remembered most of what Coach had said whenever there was a test.

Trino watched Coach move around the room, returning the other tests. It didn't take big brains to know this man had been involved in sports all his life. He wasn't fat, and he never tripped over the backpacks or books that ended up on the floor between the desks. He always wore something that had a sports team name on it. Today it was a blue-collared shirt with the silver star of the Dallas Cowboys football team above the pocket.

"We're moving into the Texas Revolution chapters," he said, as he gave back the last test. "There are a lot of people involved, so it'll be important to keep the names straight."

"What names?" some girl asked.

"Have you ever heard of Davy Crockett and Jim Bowie?" Coach replied.

"Sure, the Alamo stuff, right? My father was watching that old movie on Cable last week," a boy said.

"So, tell me, Hector," Coach Treviño said. "Did that Alamo movie happen to mention Lorenzo de Zavala or Juan Seguín?"

"Who were they?"

"Heroes of the Texas Revolution, Hector. There were *tejanos* who wanted independence from Mexico."

A boy's voice from the back called out, "Did they play *tejano* music, too?"

Trino saw Coach Treviño laugh when everyone else did. Then the man turned back to his desk and picked up another stack of papers. He waved the papers in his hands as he spoke.

"I've decided it's time for you students to get more involved in discovering the facts about the people who made history in our state."

Everyone groaned as Coach gave each person in the front desk of each row a few papers to distribute to the students behind him or her.

Trino took a paper and flipped it over to the back side. It was blank, and he started to draw *Tic-Tac-Toe* lines on it. He and Zipper usually started to play whenever Coach Treviño gave out a sheet. A cold feeling slithered down Trino's body, making his hand shake. *What's wrong with you? Zipper's not here to play Tic-Tac-Toe. He's dead.*

Trino flipped the sheet back. He started to fill his head with the names on the page just to keep thoughts of Zipper away. Then he glanced up and tried to catch whatever Coach Treviño was saying.

"You'll have about two weeks before the first pair of students has to give their report on one of the people on this list. I'll take the next two Wednesdays and give you time in our school library for research, but you should try to get to the public library on your own."

One of the girls waved her hand at Coach. "Can we choose our own partners?"

"No." He shook his head. "Next time, I'll let you choose partners. Let me read off your names and then I'll give you the rest of class to talk to your partner about your report."

Looking around the room, Trino felt a sick feeling in his stomach. He hated doing extra work, especially when he had to do it in the library. Whenever Zipper, Rogelio, and Trino had gone into the library, the lady in charge always picked on them. She always blamed them if anything went wrong with the computers, or if some book was put back in the wrong place. Once she had sent them to the vice-principal because Rogelio couldn't stop sneezing and he and Zipper couldn't stop laughing about it.

"Trino? Trino!"

Coach Treviño's loud voice made Trino stop thinking about his old friends and look up at his teacher.

"Trino?"

"Yeah?"

"Did you hear me? I said that you're working with Hector. The two of you will report on José Antonio Navarro, okay?"

Trino looked down the row as Hector looked behind him to where Trino sat. Hector's round face seemed very serious as he eyeballed his new "partner."

Trino merely raised his eyebrows. *No problem.* Hector was a school type. Trino would just let him do all the hard work.

After all the partners were announced, Coach said he'd let the students talk with their partners until the bell rang. Hector walked to the back of the classroom where Trino sat. He paused by the empty desk in front of Trino, the place where Zipper had once sat, but then he walked around the row and sat in the empty desk across from Trino.

"Hey, Trino," Hector said.

Trino only acknowledged him with a slight shrug of the shoulders. It was all he had gotten from Hector yesterday outside Epifaño's store.

"So, you know anything about this guy Navarro?"

Trino just shrugged again.

"Hey, it's okay to talk, you know."

Trino turned to look at Hector. "You didn't talk to me yesterday."

Hector's dark eyebrows crunched together. "Yesterday? Oh—yeah—by Epifaño's store." It was his turn to shrug his shoulders. "Didn't know you wanted to talk, that's all."

Trino hadn't known he wanted to talk either. What did he expect? He had never talked to school types like Hector before. Everything felt so screwed up right now. Trino had always depended on Zipper and Rogelio to hang out with, even if the three of them weren't big talkers.

Hector scratched his neck, then said, "Listen, Trino, I know you probably wanted someone else for a partner. Uh—we never worked together—or hung out—like you did with—well, you know. Uh—you know what I'm saying?"

Trino looked at Hector as he stumbled over words, trying not to mention Zipper. Trino didn't want to talk about
him either, so he said, "Listen, man, I hate talking in front
of the class, and I hate doing stupid stuff like reports."

Hector smiled, showing a mouthful of silver braces on
his teeth. "I hear you, man. I hate it, too."

Surprised by Hector's response, Trino said, "I thought
you were a school type. You always answer Coach's questions in class."

Hector leaned closer and said in a lower voice, "I
answer Coach's questions because I want to get off the
bench and get more time on the basketball court, that's all.
You play B-ball, Trino?"

"Not much. There's no place to play where I live."

"A bunch of us play up here on weekends. On the
courts outside the gym. Can you do an outside shot well?
I'm saving up for a new basketball that will—"

"Since when did basketball get to be part of the Texas
Revolution?"

Neither boy had seen Coach Treviño wander back to
where they sat.

"I just bet, Hector, if you looked up the man I gave you
to research—let's see, who was it? Oh, yeah, José Antonio
Navarro. Look up Navarro, and I don't think there'll be
anything about a *tejano* basketball team. Trino, it's going to
be up to you to keep Hector straight. He's *poco loco* when it
comes to basketball. Have you two made plans about
who's doing what if we go to the library this week?"

"Sure, we'll use the computers and get some book
numbers. Then we go to the shelves and look for the books
on Navarro." Trino spoke as if he did library work all the
time.

The wide look of surprise in Hector's and Coach Tre-viño's eyes almost made Trino smile.

"Be cool, Coach. Hector and I got it under control."

"Whatever you say, Trino." Coach Treviño walked away, shaking his head at them.

"Are you smart or just a good liar?" Hector asked Trino.

"Both." Trino answered, feeling proud of himself.

Before the bell rang, ending history class, they talked a few more minutes about computers, basketball, and some TV show that Hector had seen.

"I'll see if I can find out anything about this Navarro guy in some books I have at home. What about you?"

"Me?" Trino's eyebrows raised.

"Don't you have books at home for school stuff?"

"Oh, yeah, sure," Trino lied. "My mom's got some stuff—from a college."

"Cool!" Hector said, then walked back to his usual spot in the front of the class to get his books.

Trino stood up, then dragged his book and a wrinkled spiral notebook from his desk. He wondered if his last lie had gone too far. Where would a boy like Trino find any college books? Well, he'd just think up another lie tomorrow.

~ ~ ~

Lunch period gave Trino a stomach-ache. The first few days after Zipper and Rogelio were gone, Trino had skipped lunch and sat outside. When he'd come home starving and not see anything to eat, he realized that it was stupid not to take the free lunch given to him at school. Lately, he had picked a place in the cafeteria at the end of a table where a bunch of seventh-grade strangers sat. He ignored their stares, gulped his food down as fast as he could, then went outside, hoping he might run into Lisana Casillas.

He still hadn't figured out why Lisana chose to be his friend. They had met in a bookstore on the day he had seen Rosca and his friends beating up Mr. Epifaño. He had run away, fearing for his life, and had hidden in the bookstore. She had talked to him that day, and continued to talk to him whenever they saw each other at school. It was because of Lisana that Trino would show up at all, especially on those bleak days when he had woken up from nightmares about Zipper's shooting.

Every day he tried to talk to Lisana before she went into English class since her classroom was three doors away from where he took English with Mrs. Palacios. Most of the time, he was told, "Get out of the hall. Get to class." His best opportunity to see Lisana came at lunch period, but he had to eat first. All the fast eating filled him with gas, and he was scared he could be talking to Lisana when he'd have to burp or worse. He knew he had to get the guts to ask her to eat her lunch with him before his guts made a loud, smelly noise he couldn't stop.

Trino was anxious to find Lisana now that he had a history project to do. Lisana loved to talk about books and school, and he could ask her about this Navarro guy. She was so smart, Trino just knew she'd know something he could use.

He felt lucky when he saw her at the outside picnic table where she liked to sit and read after the lunch period. He watched her for a moment, her shiny black hair gleaming in the sun. Her hair slipped down her shoulders and framed her thin face like the black lace *mantilla* his grandmother wore at church.

When she looked up, saw him, and smiled, a special warmth stretched across his chest. She motioned for him to come join her. He had barely taken a step when two girls carrying books in their arms came up from behind Lisana and started talking.

Trino hesitated, wanting Lisana all to himself. Then he noticed that Lisana talked to the girls, but kept turning her face back towards Trino, and he knew he couldn't just take off.

As he walked to the table where Lisana sat, the girls who were standing beside it, both stopped talking to stare at him.

"Hello, Trino. Do you know my friends, Amanda and Stephanie?"

"Hi," each of them said as Lisana gestured towards one friend, then the other.

"Hello," Trino answered. He tried to look relaxed, as if getting introduced to two girls happened everyday, but he felt like somebody had put a lighted match near his face.

"Amanda and I are partners for a report in Coach Treviño's class," Lisana said.

Trino nodded, looking again at the taller of the two girls, the one with curly light brown hair. He forced himself to talk. "I have Coach Treviño third period. My partner is Hector—" He paused and gave his attention back to Lisana. "Your friend Hector is my partner."

Lisana smiled as if she liked what he told her. "Actually, Hector is my brother's friend, but I like him, too. Just make sure he doesn't make you do all the work."

The three girls giggled, but Trino didn't hear anything funny.

Girls laugh at dumb things, he thought.

"So, do you want to work in the library today?" Amanda asked Lisana. "I know it's only open until four, but we could read through a couple of encyclopedias just to get started."

"I can stay today," Lisana answered. Then she looked at Trino. "Are you going to work in the library after school with Hector?"

The three girls stared at him. He just bet that Lisana's friends thought a boy like him didn't go to the library.

"Coach said he'd give us class time on Wednesday to work in the library. That way if we have any questions, Coach can help us. Besides I have—" Trino stopped. He was going to make himself look good by saying he had a job after school helping an old man with a broken arm, but decided not to say anything after all. Why did he have to impress these girls? What did he care if they thought he was a loser? Only Lisana mattered. He'd tell her about his job with Mr. Epifaño when they were alone.

"You have—what?" Amanda asked. Impatience filled her voice.

"Nothing. It doesn't matter now." Even though anxiety simmered inside him, he forced himself to smile at Lisana. "I was going to talk to you about my history report. Hector and I have to look up—uh—" His mind went blank. All he remembered was that the man had a Mexican name. Guerrero? Treviño? Antonio?

Lisana's friends giggled together.

"Don't you even know what person you have to research?" Amanda said, emphasizing her words with an annoying giggle sound. She looked at the girl beside her, and both of them laughed more. "How can you go to the library if you don't know who you're going to read about?"

"I know who I'm going to read about because it's written down on the paper Coach Treviño gave me," Trino said. Anger made his words slow and deliberate. "And I'll have the paper with me when I'm in the library. So will you if you're so smart."

The tall one stopped smiling. The shorter one smoothed her blonde bangs and looked down at the ground.

"Come on, Stephanie. Let's go. I'll see you after school, Lisana." The tall girl nudged her friend, and they walked off.

Trino released a slow breath as he looked at Lisana. He tried to get rid of his anger so he could be nice to her. But her dark brown eyes didn't have their usual sparkle. Was she upset because of what he said to her friends?

Suddenly three words flashed inside his head.

"José Antonio Navarro," he said, like a guy who had to answer before a game-show buzzer.

"What?"

"I have to do my history report on José Antonio Navarro."

"Amanda and I have to look up Francisco Ruiz. You weren't very nice to my friends."

What did she expect? Trino chewed on his lip. Lisana's friends weren't nice to him.

In the next moment, the outside buzzer sounded loudly. It signaled the lunch period for the seventh-grade students had ended.

Lisana sighed and stood up. "I have to leave now, Trino."

He took a step closer to her. He felt like she was on the other side of a glass door, something invisible between them. All he had wanted was to talk to her, see that smile of hers that always made him feel important. What could he do to make things good between them again?

"If you want, I can be friends with those girls," he said slowly. He looked directly into her face, hoping she would trust him.

Her eyes glided over his face, as she said, "Those girls have to be friendly to you, too. Friendship is a two-way thing, Trino."

If friendship was indeed a two-way thing, then Trino knew he had to work harder at it.

"Lisana, maybe — we could eat lunch together in the caf — so we could talk more — "

She gathered her books from the table. "Okay, Trino. You'll find me at a table near the windows. See you tomorrow."

"See you tomorrow," Trino answered, and tried to feel hopeful as she walked away.

Chapter Six

Heroes

"Did you bring your mom's college books?"

Hector had walked back to the spot where Trino sat in the back of the classroom.

Trino glanced up, slightly confused by the question. All he could think about was lunch with Lisana. He thought about her yesterday while he worked with Mr. Epifaño and kept thinking about her all evening. This morning he wore jeans that were clean and made sure his T-shirt didn't have holes.

"Hey, can I sit here?" Hector asked, motioning to the desk in front of Trino.

"I don't care," he answered. He scratched his fingers through his black hair trying to remember what else Hector had asked him.

"Hey, I like this desk. It's bigger than the one I usually sit in. Okay, so what happened? Where are your mom's books?"

"What books?"

"You said that your mom had some college books. Did you find out anything about this Navarro guy?"

Trino remembered yesterday's lies and just added one more to the pile. "I looked in her books, but didn't read anything about Navarro."

"Too bad. So what do we do next?" Hector asked him.

Trino frowned. He thought Hector was a smart guy. "I guess we need to go to the library and look around. But I can't go after school." Mr. Epifaño had already promised Trino work the rest of the week. Even two bucks a day was better than nothing.

"I got practice after school and games on Saturday."

Doing the history report was going to be a pain in the neck, Trino decided. School work was *always* a pain. Then teachers added on stupid work in the library. For what? To learn about some guy in history? "I got better things to do," Trino said, finishing his thoughts out loud.

"Me, too. But I figure if we do good on the report, I might get a better shot at starting the next game."

"If you need this report to suck up to Coach, then *you* have to find the books to do the report," Trino told Hector. "If I do the report or not, my life's the same. Why should I worry?"

"So you want *me* to do all the work?" Hector's black eyebrows crinkled over his wide nose. "Well, you're full of it. You probably don't even have college books at home. Your mom probably can't even read a kiddie book."

Trino punched his hand into the side of Hector's head as hard as he could. It jerked sideways before Hector spun around and aimed his big fist. Trino pushed it aside, using the force to push himself out of his desk. For a big kid, Hector moved very fast, and he was on his feet, too, reaching out to Trino's upper body.

"Fight! Fight!" a circle of voices yelled.

Despite the size difference, Trino rammed his head into Hector's chest. Hector fell back against their desks, scraping the wall of history maps that Coach had stuck on the side bulletin boards.

The students chanted and yelled. Trino ignored them. He had to get out from under Hector's arm, wrapped tight around his neck. He couldn't breathe. He punched hard at whatever he could. Hector grunted. Then Trino's fist scraped the wall.

Hector got a solid hit into Trino's ribs, before one voice rose above the others. The loud male voice shouted, "Break it up! Now! Trino! Stop punching! Stop it! Hector, let him go!"

Rough hands pulled Trino out and pushed Hector away. Trino felt the wall against his back and Coach Treviño's hand firmly splayed across Trino's chest, holding him there.

Panting in big, angry breaths, Hector stood behind Coach. Trino could see the anger burning in Hector's black eyes from over Coach's shoulder.

"What's going on here?" Coach Treviño's face was sweaty and red. "There's no fighting in my classroom. Trino, what's the matter with you? What's the problem here?"

Trino's lips clamped shut as he gave his teacher and his "partner" a *mal ojo* to curse them both. No matter what he said, Trino knew the blame would fall on him. He didn't care.

No one, nobody, said bad stuff about Trino's mom. Hector would know that now, no matter what else happened.

"Now, I'm going to let up, Trino. But stay against the wall, hear me?" Coach said, then slowly pulled his hand away from Trino's body.

"I saw Trino punch Hector first," a girl's voice said.

"Me, too," another girl added as two others repeated, "Me, too. Me, too."

The teacher sighed, putting his hands on his hips. He frowned at Trino, then shifted so he could see Hector, too. "Did Trino start this fight, Hector? Did he hit you first?"

"Yes, Coach," Hector answered in a quiet voice. He stared at the floor.

Trino looked behind Coach Treviño to the faces of the students behind him, staring, whispering to each other. Trino knew he'd probably get chewed out by everybody from Coach Treviño to the vice-principal. Trino was nobody, but Hector was one of Coach's athletes.

"Trino hit Hector first—got it." Coach Treviño turned his body so he could give Hector his full attention. "So what did you say that made Trino mad enough to hit you? Was it just a misunderstanding, or did you say something stupid?"

The whole classroom got quiet. Trino watched Hector swallow like a rock had slid down his throat. He looked at Coach, then at Trino, then back at Coach. "I—don't know, Coach—what I said—it was both—I guess."

"Sounds like one of you said something stupid and the other did something stupid. Makes you both at fault as far as I'm concerned. Hector, you and I are going to talk about extra laps at practice today." He turned back to Trino and pointed at him. "Trino, I'll see you in the gym after school today. And—I don't plan to change anything. You two are *still* partners in this class."

Hector walked back to the front of the classroom where he usually sat. Trino ignored the two desks the fight had shoved into the wall, and sat down in the last desk in the row. He had never been in a fight in this school, but he had seen enough of them to expect his teacher to drag him to the vice-principal's office and face suspension from school.

So Trino was shocked when Coach handled everything the way he did. Probably Coach didn't want Hector in trouble with the office. But Trino? He could only wonder what Coach would tell him after school.

～ ～ ～

Trino looked over the cafeteria tables. He didn't see Lisana anywhere. He decided to get his food tray and find his own place near the windows. He didn't wait long before Lisana appeared on the other side of the table with a metal tray in her hands, too.

"It's been a terrible day! I lost my homework, got ink on my pants, and forgot my lunch at home." She put down her tray and sat down. "How's your day been going?"

Trino decided to be honest. "Not so good." He paused a moment, then said, "I had a fight with Hector during history class. I have to see Coach Treviño after school today." He tried to sound casual, and left out the part about the punching.

"A fight, huh? What did you two fight about?" Lisana opened up her milk carton.

"Hector said—something stupid—that's all."

"Hector often says something stupid," she said. "Whenever he's at our house, he always tries to annoy me. Just ignore him. That's what I do."

Trino nodded, and hungrily began to eat his lunch. He noticed Lisana ate the bread roll first. He liked to save his bread roll for last. The cafeteria ladies baked them soft and delicious. He saw Lisana take a bite out of the meat, macaroni, mixed vegetables, and pudding. She made a face each time.

"I guess you don't like the food much," he said.

"Do you want any of this? Really, it's terrible to toss it in the trash since you seem to like the food."

"I just eat it because it's free. My mom's out of a job right now."

"I'm sorry." Lisana looked down at her tray, as if she was embarrassed.

"Nothing to feel sorry about," Trino said in a normal voice. "It's just the way it is. This guy she knows — Nick — said there was a job he knew about at some college, but she doesn't want to take it."

"At a college? Is your mom a teacher?"

Trino was glad that they had shared important secrets with each other. She knew about Rosca, and he knew about Lisana's mom dying on her birthday. He trusted her not to make fun of him. "My mom works in motels and hotels — she cleans rooms and sometimes serves food at a hotel party."

"I bet she meets some interesting people," Lisana replied. She smiled. "Someday, I want to work in a place where a lot of different people come and go all the time."

Trino never thought his mom's job would be interesting in any way. Lisana was weird to think so, but he didn't tell her that. Instead, he said, "I want to learn how to fix things that are broken. Machines — maybe cars, too."

"You should meet Earl. He's my sister's husband. He can fix anything."

Lisana reached over to Trino's empty tray and swapped it with her own.

Her actions didn't surprise him. The only thing he could do for her was to hold out his bread roll. "Here, you can have my bread."

"You're nice. Thanks." She tore off pieces of the roll and put them into her mouth as she talked. "Earl built Jimmy a skateboard. He carved the board and everything."

Trino decided to eat the rest of Lisana's lunch since he was still hungry.

"Can Earl fix a broken TV?"

Lisana swallowed before she said, "I bet he could. He's got more tools than a Super K-Mart. You should see our garage."

Trino took another swallow of macaroni before he said, "I'd like to come to your house again. Uh — to meet Earl — see the garage — whatever you want to do."

Lisana's eyes sparkled as she grinned at him. He figured she might have offered him a better invitation if three girls had not approached the table to talk to her.

Trino knew them all. He recognized Amanda and Stephanie from yesterday. Lisana's runt friend, Janie, was also with them. He had met Janie at the bookstore when he had met Lisana. But Janie always got on Trino's nerves.

Today Janie was dressed completely in black, complete with painted black fingernails. Trino thought that all she needed was a bag for Trick-or-Treat and a broom.

"Wow, Lisana. You ate all that food? Gah, it was so gross," Janie said, then looked at Trino, who was trying hard not to show the girls how annoyed he felt since they showed up. "Hello, Trino. I hadn't seen you in a while. I figured you got hauled off to juvenile hall with your homeboys."

Janie always said dumb things. Trino wondered why Lisana called her a friend. He decided to follow Lisana's suggestion and just ignore people who said "stupid things." Instead, he looked at Amanda and Stephanie and tried to smile at them. They turned sideways, looking as if they only wanted to speak to Lisana.

"I thought we were going to meet in the library at lunch period, Lisana. I told you that I couldn't stay after school today," Amanda said.

"Yes, I know. I'm finished eating now." Lisana gave Trino a look that matched her words. "I'm sorry, Trino, but I have to go." She started to stand up, but then sat down and grinned at him. "But—oh! I just wanted to tell you something important."

Trino straightened up in his chair, despite the trio of girls staring at him like he was a roach on the cafeteria floor. "Something important?"

"Yes!" Lisana looked very excited. He wanted to be excited, too.

"Trino, didn't you tell me that the person for your history project was José Antonio Navarro?"

"Yeah, that's right. Navarro." Trino tried to keep the disappointment out of his voice.

"When Amanda and I were doing our research yesterday, we found out that José Antonio Navarro and Francisco Ruiz were the only *tejanos* who signed the Texas Declaration of Independence. Isn't that cool?"

"Cool," Trino said, but saw nothing "cool" about dead men in Texas history.

She reached over and pressed her hand on his arm. His skin tingled. He raised his arm so he could feel her skin even better.

"If I find out anything about Navarro that you can use in your report, I'll let you know, okay?" She stood up from the table, taking her hand away from his arm.

Trino wanted to grab it and yell out, *Don't leave. Stay here and talk to me.*

He sat there and gave Lisana a limp wave as she left with the other girls.

≈ ≈ ≈

Trino was glad he had P.E. in the gym seventh period. It would be easy to find Coach Treviño right after school. He hoped Coach would yell at him quickly, so he wouldn't be too late for work with Mr. Epifaño.

He made eye contact with his teacher in the boys' locker room. Coach motioned him over and led the way into the Coaches' office. It was a small room with three glass walls. The other wall was painted bright green and had a big bulletin board attached to it. Team schedules, school memos, and a variety of other papers spread across the board and down the wall. The desk where Coach sat was stacked with papers, too. He pointed at a black metal chair for Trino to sit in.

"Trino, do you have a problem with Hector Mendoza?" Coach Treviño asked. His voice was calm and his brown face looked teacher-serious.

Trino wasn't sure what to say. It was easier when people yelled at him for doing something stupid and he just told them he wouldn't do it again.

Coach leaned forward behind the desk, his long arms resting on the stacks of papers. "Trino, do you remember what I told you when Zipper died? I asked you if you wanted to talk to a counselor and you said you didn't want to. What about now? Do you need to talk to one?"

Trino realized what Coach meant. Now he understood why Coach didn't send him to the office. He had usually been pretty cool with Zipper and Trino. Coach liked to have a little fun with them by teasing Zipper about his clothes or asking Trino if he combed his hair with a hedge trimmer. One time Coach had shared a handful of jelly beans with the two of them that one of the other teachers had given him as a joke.

Trino felt bad he had started the fight in Coach's class. He was a cool teacher. And since Trino wanted at least one teacher to like him, he decided to tell the truth. "Hector just said something about my mom. That's why I hit him. It didn't have anything to do with Zipper. I'm okay, Coach. I don't need a counselor."

"He said something about your mom, huh? I could have put money on that." He shook his head, but then something behind Trino caught his gaze. "There's the other one, now." He sat up and gestured with his hand. "Come in, Hector. We were just talking about you."

Trino looked up as Hector came in. The boy was already dressed in a basketball jersey and loose shorts for practice.

"Tomorrow I'm taking the class to the library," Coach Treviño said. "You two start a fight in there, and I'll fry your butts good. Understand?"

Both Trino and Hector nodded.

"Tomorrow I want each of you to come into class with a list of ten questions about José Antonio Navarro. It's been two days, and I bet neither of you knows anything about him."

Trino raised his head up and said, "I know who he is. He's one of the *tejanos* who signed the Texas Declaration of Independence."

Coach Treviño raised one black eyebrow. "Hmmm. I guess it's a start. Hector, seems to me you've got a clever partner here. Don't mess it up, okay?"

"Sure, Coach," Hector said, his voice sounding deeper than usual.

Coach Treviño stood up and clapped his hands. "And just so you two don't think you got off easy, you're both going to clean out the concession stand tomorrow after school. I have a faculty meeting and have to reschedule practice anyway. I'll tell Mr. Flores, the janitor, he's going to have two strong helpers tomorrow. Any questions?"

Both boys shook their heads.

"Hector, start the boys with their laps around the court. Trino, I'll see you tomorrow. Don't be late for my class, okay?"

Trino nodded, and then followed Hector out of the coaches' office. They had just reached the metal door to the locker room when Hector stopped and turned to Trino.

"Hey, I was wrong about you, Trino."

Trino raised his eyebrows. "Yeah?"

"I just figured you were a good liar. Now I can tell you're smart. See you tomorrow, Trino."

"Later," Trino replied as Hector went into the locker room.

Trino stood there in the hallway a moment, soaking in Hector's words. A school-type had called him "smart." A flicker of pride made him stand up straight and press his shoulders back. Here was a different reputation for Trino Olivares, but so far, Trino liked the way it fit him.

Chapter Seven
Working Man

While Trino mopped the floors, took out trash, and opened boxes, he wondered how to tell the old man that he couldn't come to work the next day. He started to regret ever punching Hector at all. Tomorrow he'd be working hard, but not getting any money for it.

It was almost five when he finished re-stocking the canned goods. He waited until Mr. Epifaño had finished with a lady customer before he stepped up to the counter. "I can't come to work for you tomorrow, Mr. Epifaño. There's this school project and—uh—I need to meet with um—my partner tomorrow—uh—after school."

The old man wiped his sweaty brow with his good arm. "What's this? *¿No quieres trabajo?*"

"I want to work, but I can't tomorrow. I got some stuff I have to do," he said, then added, "for school—*para la escuela.*"

Mr. Epifaño grunted, then turned his back on Trino as he straightened up the cigarette boxes on the rack behind him. "I got *mucho trabajo*. My arm's wrapped up. It still hurts me a lot."

Trino sighed, and carried an empty box back into the storeroom. He collected the other empty ones to flatten them so they would fit better in the dumpster. He ripped up the boxes and stomped on them good before he took them outside. If only he could leave the store through the back way, but he had to get his pay. He locked up the back door, and returned to Mr. Epifaño at the counter.

"Can I have today's pay now? I need to get home."

Mr. Epifaño grunted again and opened the cash register. He pulled out two bills and handed them to Trino. One dollar bill was blue, as if it got washed in a pocket of blue jeans. The other bill had red marker scribbled across it.

"If you can't work for me regular, I'll find another boy."

Trino didn't answer as he stuck the colored money into his pocket. He didn't think anybody else would be dumb enough to work for two bucks, but he couldn't be sure the old man wouldn't do what he said.

"It's just for tomorrow, Mr. Epifaño. I'll be back the next day."

"Can you work Saturday?"

Trino hesitated. What if Nick needed Trino? How could he pass up twenty bucks?

But Nick hadn't been around lately. If Trino's mom had chased him off for good, Trino wouldn't have a job. He decided just to say, "I'll ask my mom and let you know on Friday, okay?"

"*Bueno.* I'll see you on Friday."

Trino's head ached all the way home. The pain didn't get any better when he walked inside the trailer.

"It's mine, Gus."

"Want to play with it, Beto. Beto!"

Both Gus and Beto were pulling on a rubber football, trying to get it out of the other's hands.

"Mine!"

"Beto, Beto! Mommy!"

"Shut up!" Félix yelled at them. He sat on the floor, fiddling with the knobs on the broken TV.

Their mother stood at the stove, where she was stirring scrambled eggs with chunky red and brown things floating in them. "Trino, where you been? Everybody's home but you."

He walked over to the sink to drink some water. "I had to do some stuff at school," Trino said, like he always did whenever his mother questioned him on school days.

"What stuff? The school closes at four o'clock. And if you're doing school stuff, where are your books?"

Trino felt like the roof had fallen on his head. He had left his history book in Mr. Epifaño's back room. The first time he brought his history book to do some homework and what happened? He knew he had to go back for it.

"Mom, you need something from Mr. Epifaño's store? I'll go for you," Trino said, forgetting about the water and coming closer to his mother. "Do we need milk or bread? Or eggs?"

Now that he stood closer to the stove, he stared at the egg mixture in the frying pan.

"What are those brown things, Mom?"

"Mushrooms. Irene left us a can. She said they use them in eggs in the fancy restaurants." It sounded so gross, he looked at his mother's sweating face instead. "So, can I go to the store for you?"

"With what money? We need milk, but I don't got any money coming until Friday."

Trino knew what it would take to get him back to Mr. Epifaño's. "It's okay, Mom. I found some money on the street today. I'll go get us some milk. I'll be right back, okay?" And he ran out the door before his mother could say anything else.

Trino hated to use his own money to buy milk. But he had to get his books from Mr. Epifaño's. For a boy who was supposed to be "smart," Trino felt like he had done a lot of stupid things in one day.

"What!" Mr. Epifaño said, when he saw Trino come into his store.

"I forgot my books here. And I need to buy some milk for my mom," he said as he rushed past the counter to get his books first. He saw them on the shelf as soon as he went into the back room. Then he went to the other end of the store to get the milk. He was just reaching for one of the jugs, when he heard a familiar voice behind him.

"Hello, Trino."

When he turned around and saw who it was, he felt relieved. "Hey, Nick. How's it going?"

"Just working hard, like always. " Nick was dressed in a blue work shirt and dark slacks. His name tag was pinned over the pocket. "How's your Mom?"

Trino shrugged. "She's okay. I—I just came to buy some milk."

"You still got your school books with you?" He reached behind Trino to get a loaf of bread.

"Uh—yeah—I'm working on a school project after school."

Nick smiled. "I'm glad you're getting serious about school. It makes me proud to see you trying to do more than take up space on the streets."

Trino didn't answer. It was okay to be "smart," but he didn't want to be a schoolboy. "Well, uh—Nick—I got to go now." He started to walk around Nick, then paused and said, "You got any tree jobs for us, Nick?"

Nick rubbed his chin with his long fingers. He looked down at Trino. "I thought you were going to find the next tree job for us. You said you could."

Trino had temporarily forgotten about his "deal" with Nick to find the next tree job so he could take Nick's share of the money. He kept his face straight as he said, "I'm still planning to find us a tree job. I just thought you might have something already lined up."

"Not for now."

"But if you find a tree job, I'll work with you, Nick." His voice sounded too eager, but Trino was worried he might lose a way to make better money if his mother broke things off with Nick.

"I'll let you know if anything comes up," Nick said, then gestured with his arm for Trino to pass him first.

Trino walked on down the store aisle, but he felt weird having Nick walk behind him. He tried to act cool, but his head felt hot as he worried about Nick and his mom, Nick finding them another tree job, or Trino trying to find a tree job. As he reached the store counter and placed the milk jug on it, another worry crossed his mind just as Mr. Epifaño looked up from the register and stared at Trino.

"Did you say you couldn't work for me *mañana*? *¿Por qué?* I forgot." He punched in the price of the milk on the register and put out his hand for Trino's money.

Trino felt the weight of Nick's presence behind him. He tried to keep his voice steady as if everybody knew Trino was working for Mr. Epifaño.

"I just have to do something at school. I'll help you on Friday. Maybe Saturday, too." He pulled out the two colored bills he had been paid less than fifteen minutes ago and gave them to Mr. Epifaño.

The old man flipped them between his fingers and studied them. "Is this good money?"

Trino got mad. "Those are the two dollars you gave me today. When you paid me with them, I didn't ask *you* if they were any good."

The choking sounds from Mr. Epifaño's throat startled Trino until he realized that the old man was laughing. The whiskered face, yellow from old bruises, had come alive with wet eyes and a grin of crooked teeth. "*No quiero esos dólares.* When I gave these to you, I didn't want them back." He put the bills down by the milk and closed the cash drawer. "You just take the milk for your *mamá* and forget it. Keep that money. It's still good, even colored like *cascarones.*" His laughter sputtered out again as he pushed the bills across the counter.

Trino felt embarrassed. He grabbed the bills, shoved them back into his pocket, and reached for the milk jug. As he started to turn, he remembered that Nick was still behind him. Trino knew that Nick was a big *gracias* man, always saying "Thank you" to everyone, so Trino said, "Thanks for the milk, Mr. Epifaño. *Gracias.*" He said over his shoulder, "See you around, Nick."

"Hey, stick around, Trino. I'll give you a ride home," Nick said. He reached down to get a pack of gum and laid it beside the bread he was buying.

Trino waited while Nick paid Mr. Epifaño, and even smiled when Nick teased the old man in a friendly way about paying Trino with "play" money. Then Nick told Mr. Epifaño and Trino about his first job when an old farmer always paid him with pennies. Once Nick had ten dollars of pennies in his pocket and almost drowned when he went swimming in the river.

"Was that a true story you told Mr. Epifaño?" Trino asked Nick as they got into Nick's truck.

"Sure it was. I sank like a rock. When my friends discovered I had pennies in my pocket, they all helped themselves. I was swallowing water, and they were stealing my money." Nick started the truck. "It taught me not to keep all my money in the same pocket." He chuckled to himself. "For a lot of good reasons."

Trino smiled, too, then settled back into the truck seat as Nick drove away. It felt good to be riding instead of walking home with a jug of milk and his school books.

"So, how long you been working for Mr. Epifaño?" Nick asked.

"Just this week. He needs some help since his arm is broken. I—" Trino swallowed hard and looked at Nick. "I haven't told my mom about this job. When I work with you, she takes everything, and I—I just need some money for me."

Nick had stopped the truck for a red light. He used the pause to look at Trino. "I understand, Trino. Sometimes, a man needs to help himself before he can help anybody else." Then he turned back to look up at the light, and spoke as if he was thinking out loud. "Sometimes a woman needs to help herself, too."

Trino knew who Nick was talking about. "You want Mom to take that job at the college, don't you?"

"I've been working there for two months now," Nick said. "The pay isn't bad to start, and there's overtime if you want it. I like the men I work with, and the college kids are friendly enough. I think your mom would like it there, too. I just don't understand why she won't apply."

"I don't know," Trino said, even though he had a good idea since he had heard his mom talking to Irene.

"Are you coming inside?" Trino asked as Nick pulled his truck into the trailer park.

"No, I don't think so. Just tell your mom—well, never mind." Nick shifted the truck into park, then reached into his pocket. He pulled out a few wrinkled bills.

Trino watched him peel away a pair of one dollar bills. He extended them to Trino. "Here, I'll trade you. Two regular dollars for your *cascarón* ones."

"What will you do with dollar bills like these?" Trino asked, but was glad to pull them out of his pocket and switch them with those Nick had.

"I can exchange them at the bank for better-looking bills. It's no big deal." He folded the colored money and put it back into his shirt pocket. "Two bucks isn't much, but it's a start, Trino."

"I know. I just wish it was two hundred."

Nick smiled. "I hear you, man."

"Thanks, Nick. And thanks for the ride, too," Trino said, before he opened up the truck door and stepped out.

"Hey, Trino!"

"Yeah?" Trino leaned his head through the truck window.

"If Mr. Epifaño wants you to work a full day on Saturday, you settle on your pay before you start working, okay? Don't be greedy with the old man. But let him know you expect more money if he wants you for a full day. And then you give him all you've got to earn it."

Trino nodded, knowing that he was going have to speak up for himself since there would be no one else to do it. As he watched Nick drive away, Trino realized that there were a lot of things that Nick Longoria could teach him—things that weren't taught in school.

He tried to stay hopeful that Nick would come back to their house again, as he carried the milk and his books inside the trailer house.

"Did I see Nick's truck?" his mom asked as soon as Trino stepped inside. She stood near the stove, warming tortillas on a *comal*. "Is he coming inside?"

He put the milk jug on the table, where his three brothers were already seated and eating eggs and buttered bread. He noticed that each plate had a pile of brown mushrooms pushed off to the side. He had to smile, because he knew he'd probably do the same thing.

"Nick gave me a ride back from Mr. Epifaño's, that's all. Is there any supper left for me?"

Trino tossed his history book and notebooks on the sofa and went to sit at the table.

"We're out of bread. But I saved you a few tortillas. Did — uh — did Nick say anything important?"

Trino looked at his mother's anxious face, then noticed his brothers' curious ones. He wanted to say something about the job at the college, but decided she might get mad. "Nick just gave me a ride home. That's all, Mom."

"Will you work with him this Saturday?" She came to the table with scrambled eggs and two tortillas on a plate. She set it down in front of Trino. "We could use the money right now."

"He said he didn't have work for me this week," Trino said.

His mother's shoulders dropped as she walked back to the stove. He wondered if she missed the money Trino could make, or if she was sad because Nick hadn't come back.

Trino said nothing else, as he started to pick the mushrooms out of his eggs with his fingers.

❧ ❧ ❧

"What are you doing? Trino, it's late. Go to bed." His mother's tired voice came from behind him.

History book opened in front of him, Trino sat at the kitchen table, trying to come up with three more questions about José Antonio Navarro. It had taken him a long time to write each question neatly. He searched through his book, trying to find more information about the man, but gave up. He guessed that's why Coach was letting them use books in the library.

"I'm trying to write down ten questions about this man. It's for a school project. I just can't think of anything else." He looked over his shoulder. "Can you help me, Mom?"

She sighed loudly, but still came over to the table. "What are you doing?"

"You see, this guy, José Antonio Navarro, was one of the *tejanos* who signed the Texas Declaration of Independence."

"I don't know anything about that stuff, Trino. Ask your teacher," she said with an impatient wave. Still, she sat down at the table beside him.

"What I have to do tonight is write down ten questions — stuff I want to know about this man. But you know, Mom? I don't care about this guy. I wish teachers wouldn't give us all the stupid stuff to do. That's why I don't like school."

"*Ay, mijo,* you sound just like me when I was your age. Now, I wish I had paid attention. Learned how to read good — then I could get a better job." She reached over and picked up the pencil he had put down. She flipped it between two fingers as she talked. "You need to try and learn this stuff that the teachers want, Trino. So you can be smart—book smart. Then you'll get a job that doesn't break your back."

Her eyes focused upon her son's face. "Look at Nick. He's always thinking of better ways to do something. He knows how to use his *cabeza*. When he was in charge at the motel where I worked, everything ran so smooth. Now he's working at a college and doing his tree jobs. He likes what he does and where he works. I wish I could be like him."

"Nick wants you to work with him at the college," Trino replied. "That's what he told me today. He said you would like it there, Mom."

She laid the pencil on the table, placing her hand flat upon it. She chewed on her lip, lowered her eyes, but said nothing to Trino. He saw an unfamiliar look on her face, but couldn't quite name it.

"Nick told me today that sometimes a man—a person—has to help himself before he can help others."

"Why would he say that to you?"

Trino hesitated, then said, "I don't know, Mom, he just did."

Slowly, his mother put her hand on the open history book, then looked up at Trino. "When I go looking for a job, I get asked a lot of questions. Mostly about where I've worked before—stuff like that. This guy—the one you want to write about for school—maybe you could find out what jobs he did before he signed—whatever it was he signed—" She smiled a little.

"What about his family—*la familia*—who were they? Were they rich people, or was he a man from the barrio?"

"That's good, Mom. I can write down those questions. I just need one more." Trino wrote down, *Who was his family? Was he a rich tejano?*

"Do you have any other ideas?"

"*Pues*, I don't know. Why did he sign—what did you say it was called?"

"The Texas Declaration of Independence, Mom."

"Oh! Well—what happened after he signed it? I mean, sometimes when I sign a paper I get something good. Sometimes I sign a paper and I owe more money. Was he glad he signed it? That's something you could ask."

"That's good, Mom." Trino wrote down, *What happened after Navarro signed the declaration?* He looked up and smiled. "Thanks for helping me."

She reached over and rustled her fingers through his black hair. She smiled back at him. "It felt good to help you, *mijo*."

~ ~ ~

"These are good questions, Trino." Coach Treviño looked up from Trino's notebook and then looked over the paper that Hector had brought in. "Yours are good, too, Hector. If you two can find the answers to these questions, your report will fall right into your hands."

Trino and Hector looked at each other. He just knew Hector was thinking the same thing, *Yeah, right.*

As Coach Treviño started to circle the library where other students looked through books and sat at the computers, Hector motioned at Trino to follow him towards the encyclopedias.

"You start with the 'N' books. I'm going to read through the 'T' books. Maybe one of us will find something," Hector said, and started moving his fingers over the tall books on the bottom shelf.

Trino saw all the kids bunched up around the computers and wondered if they would get finished faster than Hector and him. If he came to school early tomorrow, would the librarian show him how to use the computer better? She hadn't been nice before, but this time he wouldn't have Zipper and Rogelio with him. Thinking of his old friends, he felt sad.

Then he saw Hector thumbing through a book for their report. He remembered Coach Treviño's words of praise. Trino knew he could change the way people thought of him. Even if those changes happened one person at a time.

Chapter Eight
The Guys

"Man, I like to eat *nachos,* but scraping this cheese off the shelves is really gross!" Hector said, as he flicked up lumpy layers of hardened cheese with a dull knife.

The concession stand was really a cramped side room at the entrance of the gym. A tall wooden counter served as a front wall, with shelves, a plastic sign with prices for snacks and sodas, and a broken digital clock hanging behind them on the rear wall.

For the past hour, Trino's job had been to organize the soda canisters, separating the full ones from the empties. He had stacked boxes of paper products, cans of unopened cheese, and jars of big pickles under the counter. Then he would sweep and mop the floors. The janitor had ordered Hector to clean off the shelves—first scraping off anything left behind, then washing them down.

But one thing Trino had learned about his "partner" was that when Hector was talking, he wasn't working. Hector had started talking about the basketball team first, then he moved on to TV shows, and found a way to bring up food he liked to eat. Trino was ready to sweep and mop, but Hector hadn't washed down the shelves yet.

"Can't you work any faster?" Trino asked him, standing up from his kneeling position. He stretched his back and shoulders, stiff from bending under the counter. "I can't sweep if you're dropping junk on the floor."

"It's hard doing what I'm doing," Hector replied. He gritted his teeth as he slid the knife under another layer of dried cheese. "Man, is this stuff made of glue or what? Ugh!"

The cheese flipped up from the shelf and went flying in Trino's direction.

"Hey!" Trino slapped away the chunk, and it went back in Hector's direction.

Hector popped it with the knife, and it flew by Trino's face. "What do you know? Cheese volleyball!"

When Trino didn't try to hit it back, Hector frowned. "Aw, man, lighten up. I was just having a little fun."

"This isn't fun. It's work, Hector. And I got better stuff to do than pop cheese back in your face. Hurry up, so you can start washing the shelves and I can sweep and mop," Trino answered, feeling impatient and irritated with Hector's silliness.

"Jeez, you sound like my mother," Hector grumbled. He turned his back on Trino and went back to sliding the knife under dried cheese lumps. He started talking about cleaning his room last week and his mother's peculiar way of vacuuming a carpet.

"I'll be back. I'm going to go fill the bucket with soap and water," Trino said.

He figured if Hector had no one to talk to, maybe he'd work faster. Trino grabbed the bucket the janitor had left out and headed towards the closet door marked *Maintenance* across the way. The janitor had left the door propped open with a thick block of wood. Trino opened the heavy door and put on the light switch. He lifted the bucket into the deep sink against the back wall and turned on the faucets. He recognized the bottle of floor cleaner on the shelf above him. It was the same kind his mother had brought home from the motels to clean their floors. He poured a generous amount into the water, then watched the bubbles foaming their way to the top of the bucket.

"Hey, Trino, you seen the broom?" Hector kicked the block of wood with his foot. It slid across the floor of the closet. "Let's play some hockey!"

"Hector!" Trino yelled, just as the heavy door shut behind Hector's startled face. "The door, you idiot! That block of wood was keeping the door open!"

Hector waved him off. "Don't have a heart attack. They just don't want anyone getting inside. We can get out with no problem. See—" He turned back and tried the door-knob.

"Ugh—you see—" He squeezed and twisted the knob. He jumped backwards when the metal knob fell off and clanged on the cement floor.

Trino dropped his head into his hand. He couldn't believe anyone could be so stupid.

"Oh, man! Aw, hey! Hey!" Hector started pounding on the metal door. "Hey! Hey! Can anybody hear me? Hey! Help! Help us! Oh, man! Man, we're trapped in here. Help!"

Trino heard the panic rising in Hector's voice. He shut off the water and went towards the door. "Hey, Hector, relax—"

"Naw, you don't understand." Hector shoved his shoulder into the door. "I can't be inside a place like this." He banged himself against the door again. And again. "It makes me crazy. Trino, we've got to get out of here." His sweaty face and wild-eye look shocked Trino. Hector was the kind of guy who was usually silly, smiling and laughing.

"What if we get trapped here all night long? Trino, I can't breathe. There's no air in here." He wrapped his hands around his neck. "I'm suffocating! Where is all the air?"

"Hector! Hector!" Trino grabbed the bigger boy by the arm and pulled him away from the door. "Hector! Stop pounding on the door. Let's think about this. The janitor is still around. He'll be back. He's got to put his stuff away, right? He's got to check on us, right?"

Hector shook off Trino's grip and backed against a side wall. He looked up, his eyes darting around the ceiling and walls. His fingers scraped against the wall like a caged animal, desperate to find an escape. "Gaw, it's so small in here. There's hardly any air. How come there are no windows? We need windows—so somebody can see that we're in here. What if no one finds us? Trino, I don't want to die in the janitor's closet! I can't breathe anymore. I can't!" He slid down the wall and slumped down on the floor, his body heaving with sobs.

Hector cried and kept repeating "I don't want to die" over and over. The whimpering sounded so pathetic, Trino got down on one knee to talk to him.

"Hector, listen to me. We're going to get out of here. I promise. The janitor is around somewhere. He's going to open the door soon."

Slowly, Trino reached out and put his hand on Hector's shaking shoulder. "Listen to me. This room isn't so small. It's—it's pretty big, actually. My bedroom at home is smaller than this, and I share it with two brothers."

"Really?" Hector lifted his head, his eyes wet, his nose slimy with mucus. "How can you live in a little room like that?"

"It's all we've got, that's all. Tell me about your house, Hector. Where do you live?"

"I—I live in a house by—by the Dairy Cream. On Santa Clarita—you know where that is?"

"Yeah. It's not too far from where I live. What does your house look like?"

"Uh—well—purple—it's a purple house. My dad hates the color, but my—" He paused and drew in a deep breath. "My mom is an artist—and she wanted our house to be different—I don't like to invite the guys to my house—because—aw, Trino—don't tell anybody I live in a purple house, please—"

Trino smiled at him. "I won't say anything, man. Tell me about your mom and dad. Are they cool?"

He kept Hector talking, answering as many little dumb questions as Trino could think of. It helped keep Hector calm, but it also made Trino realize that he and Hector had things in common. Hector had three younger brothers, he didn't really like school that much, and he wished he had more spending money. But the biggest surprise came when Hector admitted that he like Lisana Casillas, his best friend's sister.

"Don't you think that Lisana is pretty?" Hector asked Trino.

"Yeah, some. She's okay," Trino answered, although it became difficult for him to breathe.

"When we're hanging out at Jimmy's house, I pick on her all the time just so she'll notice me." Hector's face had dried up, and his voice was almost back to normal. "The bad thing is that she likes to read books and stuff. Ugh, and that poetry junk she drags us to hear at the bookstore. Well, you know, Trino. I once saw you there. Did you like that stuff?"

Trino hated to admit that he had enjoyed the last time he went with Lisana to hear a writer talk. It gave them something special to talk about, a connection that he shared with no one else. They hadn't been able to talk about anything like that in weeks, not until this history report stuff came up. He could probably use the assignment to spend more time with Lisana if he planned it right. But what about Hector? Now that Trino knew his partner liked the same girl he did, Trino would have to figure out how to spend time with Lisana without Hector around.

A pounding on the metal door from the other side put Lisana completely out of Trino's mind.

"Anybody in there?"

"Mr. Flores! Mr. Flores!" Both boys yelled together as they got up from the floor.

Hector's big fist pounded on the door. "Get us out of here!"

They heard the jingle of keys, then the door opened. Mr. Flores, a fat man in a gray uniform, looked at them with an angry frown.

Hector just rushed out of the closet and into the open area near the concession stand. He gulped in air like he had been holding his breath underwater.

"What's wrong with you boys? Didn't you see that chunk of wood I keep as a doorstop? And what t'hell happened to the doorknob?" the janitor wanted to know.

"Hector kicked the block by accident, Mr. Flores," Trino said. "When the door slammed, it knocked the knob off. We knew you'd be back and would get us out." He spoke as if being trapped in a janitor's closet with a guy who went crazy in small spaces happened to him every day. He almost laughed at the relief on Hector's face.

"Well, you boys need to finish up here. I got better things to do than babysit the two of you. Grab that mop and the broom and get that bucket of soap out of my sink. And see this? I'm putting this block here. One of you holds the door open while the other one's inside, get it?" Mr. Flores jammed the block of wood into place. As the janitor walked off, they heard him cussing at the school district because they wouldn't buy a modern door with a release bar so nobody got trapped inside the storeroom.

Hector ran to the door and held it wide open. "Trino, you can get the supplies out of the room. I'll wait here."

Trino stared hard at Hector. "I just saved your butt, and you want me to do all the work? It's your fault for kicking that stupid block. And if it hadn't been for me, you'd have been a crying baby when Mr. Flores let us out."

"Hey, hey, I know, I know." Hector raised his hands as he spoke, but his back was firmly planted against the open door. "Trino, everything you said is true. All of this is my fault. I never should have said anything about your mom and started our fight. I shouldn't have played kickball with that block of wood. I broke the door handle, too. Hey, man, if you want, I'll do all the rest of the work. I'll sweep, I'll mop, I'll even shine your shoes. Only — Trino — man — I just can't go back into that closet. I just can't."

Trino could have teased Hector, called him a chicken, but in the thirty minutes or so he had been stuck with Hector, he had come to like the guy. And it wasn't fair to use Hector's fear against him. Hector couldn't help being scared of small spaces just like Trino couldn't help that he had black hair.

"Okay," Trino said, ready to take full advantage of Hector's offer. "I'll get all the supplies out, and you can finish the job by yourself. Then I'll put everything back in the closet."

"Sure, yeah, great."

Trino got the mop and broom out, then went back for the bucket of mop water. He set it down by the concession stand and watched Hector sweep the floor.

"Hey, you forgot to wipe down the shelves," Trino said. "Let me find a rag or sponge and you can do that, too."

"Thank you for being *so-oo* helpful," Hector said after Trino tossed a hard sponge onto one of the back shelves. He turned and gave Trino a grin and cross-eyed look, and both boys broke up with laughter.

By the time Coach Treviño returned from his teachers' meeting, Hector had finished cleaning, and Trino had put everything back into the closet.

"Hey, this place looks good. The last pair of clowns who did this job broke a pickle jar and got stuck in the janitor's closet because they let the door slam behind them," Coach Treviño said, shaking his head and grinning. "Who could be that dumb, huh?"

Hector and Trino exchanged a little smile before Trino said, "Can we go now, Coach?"

"Sure, guys. I'll see you tomorrow in school."

～ ～ ～

Friday, after history class, Hector made a quick comment before he left about seeing Trino at lunch time. Trino didn't promise anything, hoping to eat with Lisana instead. He spotted her by the cafeteria windows, only she wasn't alone. A boy stood across the table talking to her, and they both looked angry. It took Trino a moment to realize that the boy was Lisana's twin brother, Jimmy.

He didn't want to lose a chance to talk to Lisana, so Trino made his way to the table and left an empty spot between his chair and where Lisana sat, so he wouldn't seem like an intruder.

"I'm not doing this report for you, Jimmy. No matter what you say." Lisana looked sideways when Trino arrived. "Hello, Trino. Sit down. Don't mind my blockhead brother here. He's leaving anyway."

Jimmy glanced at Trino, too, then said, "Look, Lisana, you're good at school stuff—"

"So are you! You're just being lazy. You can come with Amanda and me on Saturday to the city library—"

"But I have a scrimmage game on Saturday—"

"The game doesn't last all day, dummy. Now go away so I can eat my lunch with my friends," Lisana replied, then grabbed an apple beside her brown lunch bag and took two big bites. She turned herself to face Trino, but she had to attempt a swallow before she could talk.

Trino smiled. She looked funny with her face stuffed with apple. He decided to help her out by talking first. "Hector and I are having a tough time doing our report, too. There's nothing in the school books about Navarro. When Hector complained to Coach today, he said that it's because the white men who wrote the history books left out the *tejanos*. He said we need to find books written by *latinos* if we want to get better information."

Finally Lisana had chewed enough so she could talk. "Maybe we should go to Maggie's bookstore and look around. She has more books by *latinos* than I've ever seen at a library."

Trino's eyes widened. "You mean *buy* books for this report?"

"Well, no. I just thought we might see the titles, maybe read a little. I don't think Maggie would mind. Do you, Jimmy?" She looked back at her brother.

Jimmy sighed, as if to release his earlier anger. He pulled out the cafeteria chair across from them and sat down. "Well, Maggie's cool and all—but it would be kind of like cheating her if we used her books like she was a library." His dark eyes moved from his sister to Trino. "I guess I got it easier than you two. At least Burnet was an Anglo guy. It hasn't been too hard to find books about him. But I still don't know how to organize it. And Coach paired me up with Mario. He misses a lot of school because of his asthma. I feel like I'm doing this report all by myself." He reached across the table and swiped some potato chips from the open bag near Lisana's sandwich.

"Hey! That's my stuff. If you're too lazy to get up and make your own lunch, don't steal mine!" Lisana told him, as she pulled her chips and sandwich closer to her.

"Relax! I'm going to get a tray. The cafeteria cooks can't mess up hamburgers too bad, can they, Trino?" Jimmy said.

Trino was glad that Jimmy included him in the conversation. He hated when people acted like he wasn't even there.

"Hey! My man, Hector," Jimmy said, looking beyond Trino's shoulder at someone else. "And look it there! He's got two hamburgers on his tray. One's for me, right? Your best friend since childhood, right?"

"Wise up, Casillas! We've only been friends since last year. And if you think I'm parting with half my lunch, you're nuts, man. I had to pay the cafeteria extra for a second hamburger."

Hector put his tray down between Trino and Lisana. "Take one of these and you die!"

"Don't tempt him, Hector. Go sit on the other side of Trino, or I guarantee your food will be in my brother's big mouth." Very calmly, Lisana leaned over to push Hector's cafeteria tray around Trino's.

Trino continued to push Hector's tray two chairs down. "Yeah, sit over here on the other side of me, man. Away from Jimmy. You don't want him to take your food." Now that he knew Hector liked Lisana, he didn't want the guy in between them either.

But Hector sat only one chair away from Trino and pulled his tray back in front of him.

"I'll be back. If you see Albert, wave him over here too," Jimmy said, then walked off.

"Lisana, what are you doing here with the gorilla guys?"

This question came from Janie, Lisana's friend, who sat down across from Lisana with her food tray. Today, Janie was dressed completely in orange.

"Hey, Janie, doing your shopping at the Halloween Bargain Basement again? You look like a pumpkin," Hector said before taking a bite from a hamburger.

Janie just rolled her eyes and said to Lisana, "Don't you want to sit some place else?"

"No, I like it here by the windows," Lisana said. "Besides, Trino and I were talking about looking for books for Coach Treviño's report."

"I sure lucked out," Janie said. "Mr. Chaffee doesn't make us do extra stuff in his history class."

But Lisana didn't seem to be listening. "It would be so interesting to read more books written by *latinos.*" She smiled at Trino.

"There she goes again with the books stuff," Hector said to Trino, shooting the words out of the side of his mouth. "Next, it'll be poetry junk."

Trino gave Hector a nudge with his elbow to quiet him. "There's got to be some place besides Maggie's store that has the books we need."

"Hmmm." Lisana cocked her head to one side. Suddenly, her face brightened. "I know! We can go to the university. My sister told me that a college library has a lot of books for research. I bet Coach would give us extra credit if we used college books."

"Are you crazy? You think they're going to let a bunch of seventh-graders into a college library?" Hector said. He spoke with a mouthful of hamburger. Bread and meat pieces smashed together as he talked. "Besides, Trino and I don't have a library card for a college library. Do we, Trino?"

Trino wanted to say that he didn't have any kind of library card, but kept silent. He looked from the gross sight in Hector's mouth back to Lisana's annoyed expression.

"You don't need a college library card, Hector. You just stay and read the books there. You take notes from your reading. My sister used to do it all the time."

Trino thought Lisana's idea was crazy, too, but he wanted to look nicer than Hector; so Lisana would like Trino better. "I've never gone to the college library, Lisana. But I'll go with you if you think we can find books by *latinos* there."

She rewarded him with a glowing smile. "That'll be great, Trino. Thanks. I'll talk to Amanda and see if she can come with us." She looked around Trino to give Hector a questioning look. "Well? Hector, are you coming with us? You're Trino's partner, right?"

"I have a scrimmage game on Saturday. Sorry!" He gave Trino a wink. It seemed like he thought he was smart for getting out of the library trip.

"Then we'll go on Sunday—in the afternoon," Lisana said. "Jimmy can come with us, too."

Trino was relieved that Lisana picked a day when he wouldn't lose any money. But he wasn't so sure he wanted to spend Sunday afternoon in the library, either.

"I guess we should go, Trino. There might be books we can use for our report."

Hector sounded so serious that Trino just stared at him. "And then we'll get the girls to write the report for us, huh?" He gave his goofy grin and cross-eyed look to Lisana and Janie, then laughed at their reaction when both girls started to complain loudly.

Trino smiled, not because Hector was funny, but because he knew that as long as Hector said dumb things, Lisana might like Trino more.

When Jimmy came back with his food and brought the boy named Albert along, they kept joking around, talking and laughing. None of the guys made fun of Trino like they did each other. But when they did make a joke, they didn't seem to mind that Trino laughed with them. By the end of the lunch period, Trino still felt like someone standing outside a window looking in. Did he have a chance to become just another one of the guys?

Chapter Nine
Give and Take

"I finished going through the vegetable bins," Trino told Mr. Epifaño. "It's after five. I need to go home now."

The old man had been stacking packs of cigarettes in a high shelf behind the counter. "You smoke these?" he asked as he pushed the last few packs into place.

"No. They cost money I don't have," Trino answered. When he was in fifth grade, he had smoked to show off with Zipper and Rogelio. That night his mother had smelled the evidence on his clothes and whipped him with the belt. "Those cigarettes will kill you!" she had yelled as she strapped him hard. "They killed my mother, they killed my father. I got two sisters who can't talk without coughing. You live in this house—you better not smoke. You hear me? Hear me?"

Now he connected cigarettes with Rosca and his gang—they had been smoking when the plans to rob the car wash had been discussed—and that brought up memories of Zipper's dead body. No, cigarettes would be one thing Trino would never do again. Never.

"Here, boy. Pick up all these empty cartons on the floor, will you?" Mr. Epifaño kicked a carton with his foot, then hobbled over towards the counter. "*Ay*, I can't bend over, can't get my clothes on after I use the toilet—why didn't those boys just finish the job and kill me?"

"Don't say that!" Trino's reaction was loud and fierce. "You shouldn't want anyone to kill you! It was mean and ugly—what Rosca did. He beat you with a pipe! How could he do that to you? You never hurt him—never hurt anybody!"

With a sharp intake of breath, Trino realized what he had revealed.

Mr. Epifaño squinted. He rubbed his nose and said, "I got a lot of pain, boy. Sometimes, you just want to die when you feel this bad."

Trino said nothing right away. He thought the old man would ask Trino how he knew so much about what had happened, but Mr. Epifaño seemed too sad to make any connection, to realize that Trino had been a witness to the crime. In his relief, Trino also felt a keen sense of pity for what Mr. Epifaño had lived through.

"I'll pick up the boxes for you. And then I'll come back tomorrow. Do you still want me *manaña*, Mr. Epifaño?" He walked around the counter and started to gather the empty cartons into his arms. Now that he was closer he noticed Mr. Epifaño's pants drooped down near his bony hips and his shirt was unbuttoned at the bottom.

It must be tough to do things with only one good arm, he thought.

"*Manaña está bien,*" Mr. Epifaño said, hiking his pants up. "The trucks deliver about nine. Can you come *a las nueve?*"

"What will I do?" Trino felt it was only fair to ask.

"Stack the sodas, put the beer in the coolers—as that's what I sell on weekends. Lots of *cervezas—muchas cervezas.* There's a lot to do tomorrow."

Still hugging the cigarette cartons in his arms, Trino approached Mr. Epifaño about his hours and his pay, just like Nick had advised him to do. "Will you want me for a full day's work, Mr. Epifaño?"

The man's bushy eyebrows raised and lowered. Trino wasn't sure if Mr. Epifaño had understood, so he started to repeat himself in Spanish. However, the old man interrupted.

"I can use you all day, boy. I work until four. That's when my *primo* comes in and takes over. You stay 'til then, okay?"

Despite his trembling legs, Trino tried to sound like he was in charge. "When I work with another man I know, he usually pays me twenty dollars for a full day's work. What do you pay?"

Mr. Epifaño pushed out his lower lip as his eyes looked at the floor. "I don't know, boy. Twenty dollars is a lot of money. Some days *I* don't make twenty dollars." He raised his gaze and looked into Trino's face. "I can give you ten dollars for the day, boy."

It was more than Trino expected, but he didn't let any reaction show on his face. Instead, he said, "Mr. Epifaño, my name is Trino. Can you call me Trino instead of boy?" Then he smiled at the old man. "I'll be here at nine o'clock." He carried the cartons out to the dumpster, feeling so proud of himself. He wished he could tell Nick all about it, and that was the only thing that disappointed Trino about his workday.

Inside the back room, he gathered his school books together and saw the box of bruised vegetables nearby. Feeling braver by the minute, Trino went back into the store. "Mr. Epifaño, can I take home those vegetables in the box? My mom can use them for cooking."

"*Sí, sí.* Take them home. Usually, my *primo* puts them in the trash."

While he was grateful for the food, Trino's arms were stiff and sore by the time he carried the vegetables back to the trailer park.

He kicked the screen door and yelled, "Somebody open the door! My hands are full!"

"*Ay, ay, ay,*" his mother exclaimed when she pushed the screen door open and stepped aside for Trino to enter. "Where did you get all the vegetables?"

"From Mr. Epifaño," Trino said in a breathless voice. He dropped the box onto the kitchen table and sighed in relief. "Oh, my arms! I feel like I carried a pile of bricks home." He scooped his books off the top of the box and wrinkled his nose at the squashed tomato clinging to his spiral notebook. He flicked the pulp and seeds back into the box.

"Were you working for Mr. Epifaño or what?" his mother asked, eagerly reaching into the box and turning the squishy tomatoes, wilted lettuce, and other vegetables in her hands.

"I just helped him a little after school," Trino said, bending the truth as much as he could. "He gave me the box of vegetables. He was going to toss them in the dumpster anyway." He didn't add that Mr. Epifaño had given Trino a roll of nickels, too.

Trino noticed how quiet the trailer seemed. "Where is everyone?"

"Oscar picked up Félix for the weekend. Beto and Gus are staying with your Tía Sofia for the night. I'm working." His mother's voice seemed happier than he had heard her in weeks. "It's just serving a wedding and cleaning up the place afterwards, but it's a job."

"That's good, Mom," Trino said, feeling relieved he hadn't come home to the grouchy woman who usually lived in this trailer.

"I wish I had time to clean these vegetables, but I have to be at the church hall by six. Just put them on the counter and I'll chop them up when I get home." She moved away from the box and went to get her purse where she kept it on top of the refrigerator. "Trino, there's bread and peanut butter. You can cut up a few vegetables and eat those, too."

Trino nodded as he watched his mother place the purse strap over her shoulder. "I should be back after midnight. You stay home, hear me?" He kept nodding at everything she told him. As he watched her walking across the trailer driveway, he was already planning to go buy himself a juicy hamburger, even if he had to pay for it with a worn-out dollar bill and a handful of nickels.

※ ※ ※

He was awakened by the slam of a door. It took a moment to realize he had been in a deep sleep, so relaxing because his little brother wasn't beside him in the bed. Sleeping with Beto was like being in the middle of a kickball game where everyone kicked you instead of the ball. Tonight Trino had enjoyed every inch of the bed he had all to himself.

The next sound he heard was running water. Someone was in the kitchen.

Trino grabbed his shorts and slipped them over his underwear before he headed out. "Mom, is that you?"

He saw her going through the box from Mr. Epifaño's store. She took the vegetables out, rinsing some off, tossing others into the trash can. Her movements were rigid. Cuss words in both Spanish and English kept up a harsh tempo as she worked. She turned towards the kitchen drawer, saw Trino, and gasped. Her whole body skittered like she had been surprised. "*Ay*, Trino! What are you doing? Trying to kill me with a heart attack?"

"I heard noise—"

"Well, go back to sleep." She snapped off the words, then reached over to get a knife from the stove. "I got things to do."

"How come you're so mad?" he asked.

"I got things on my mind. Now go back to sleep!"

He would have followed her order, except that she kept talking. She turned back to the counter and started chopping the vegetables she had washed.

"I'm not a kid. I should have known what that man wanted."

"What man?" Trino asked, coming closer to where she stood.

She groaned, then wiped her sweaty forehead with the back of her hand. "One of the servers— a guy who mowed the grass when I was a maid at *The Brownside Motel*—he offered to take me home. It was so late, and I thought he was being nice." She stabbed the knife into a wilted head of cabbage and seemed to take pleasure in smashing it against the kitchen counter. "He stopped his car in an empty lot and started grabbing me. He's a big man—like Nick. I'm so mad! I should have taken my chances on the dark streets."

She knocked the cabbage into the sink and started ripping leaves. "And the worst part was that he took my money. I pushed him off me and got out of the car. But he followed me. He rolled down the window and threw my purse at me. Only he took out the envelope with my pay in it." She started cussing again, cursing every man who ever cheated her, talked to her — whatever.

She even made Trino feel guilty he was a man. He started to feel the weight of his mother's emotions. He got mad at himself for using three dollars for that hamburger, fries, and a coke last night. And he was mad at his mom for taking this job, then losing the money because she went home with a man she barely knew.

"I don't know what we're going to do this month for rent money," she said, but not really to Trino. "If I use all the welfare check for rent, there'll be nothing left for other stuff. But I won't have my family living on the streets, that's for sure."

Even though it made him furious, he told her, "I'm working tomorrow with Mr. Epifaño, Mom. He doesn't pay like Nick does, but you can have whatever I make."

She chopped into the potatoes and carrots like they had insulted her, and told Trino, "Whatever food Mr. Epifaño wants to throw away, you bring home. No matter what it is, you hear me?" His mother sighed and pushed her hair out of her face with the back of her hand. "I don't care if you don't like it — we got to eat whatever we can get, Trino. Hear me?"

Trino nodded. "I hear you. I'm going back to bed."

"Go throw that box outside first. It makes the kitchen stink."

When he came back inside the trailer, his mother was already in her room with the door closed. Trino went back to his bed and lay down, staring at the ceiling until sunrise.

Trino couldn't remember the last time he was so tired. He had worked harder with Nick, but he had never worked after being awake half the night. His body ached and his head pounded as he walked home with ten dollars in his pocket and a large bag of dented sodas, smashed cookie bags, two loaves of hard bread, and three jars of apricot jelly that someone had opened but then put back on the shelf. Six dented cans of soup and one torn bag of flour added more weight than Trino wanted to carry, but he did it anyway.

At the store, he had done a lot of lifting and moving boxes, rearranging sodas and beer cans in the coolers, and anything else that Mr. Epifaño wanted. The work wasn't anything Trino couldn't do. Mr. Epifaño had let him eat a package of stale donuts and a pint of milk in the morning, and have a soda and pretzels in the afternoon without charging him. Whenever Trino had found a food item that couldn't be sold, he asked for it instead of tossing it in the dumpster. At first Mr. Epifaño didn't want him to take anything, but when Trino told him that someone stole his mother's purse, the old man did look through the shelves again to see if he could add something else to Trino's bag.

Beto and Gus thought it was Christmas when Trino came in with the sodas and cookies. His mother was glad to see the bread and jelly. The house smelled good since Tía Sofia had given Trino's mom two soup bones when she had picked up the boys. Now a big pot of *caldo* simmered on the stove.

"I also got some money," Trino told her, pulling the ten-dollar bill from his pocket. Someone had drawn a little moustache on the president's face, but it was still money to give her.

"I wish it was more," she said, and stuck the bill in the back pocket of her jeans.

She had been asleep when he had left at eight-thirty. Now in the late afternoon's light, he could see bruises on her cheek from last night's episode. He walked away, hoping a hot shower would soothe the anger and tiredness out of his body.

It was the bowl of hot soup that helped Trino regain his energy, even though his mother warned them as she served the *caldo* they could have only one bowl each. Lucky for them, Irene showed up to visit. When their mother politely offered her *comadre* a bowl of soup, Irene told their mother to give the boys a little more so she wouldn't have to eat alone.

As they ate, Irene had plenty to say about their mother's bruises.

"And what can you expect, working 'til midnight, *comadre*? Now maybe you'll stop this night work. You should be at home with your boys, not serving plates to wedding guests," Irene said, then scooped a spoonful of *caldo* into her mouth.

"Don't tell me what I already know, Irene. Maybe I could get on at the candy factory—"

"Mamá, you goin' to make candy?" Beto asked. He was scooping in soup, kneeling on his chair as he ate.

"Candy? Candy? I want candy!" Gus exclaimed. He put down his spoon and held out his hand to his mother.

"You *niños* stop! There's no candy for you today. Now eat your *caldo*," their mother said in a loud voice. She reached out to slap Gus's little hand.

Beto plopped down in his chair and Gus started to whimper, but they kept eating as they were told. Trino felt bad for his brothers. At least they could share a soda later—if his mother didn't offer it to Tía Reenie first.

"*Comadre,* they're talking layoffs where I work. They always let the new people go first," Irene said. "You know how it is."

"There's the blue jean factory—"

"*Comadre,* stop being so chicken and go apply at the college like your boyfriend wants. You know that's a better job than sewing zippers on blue jeans all day long. The sewing-machine women turn hunchback and get bad eyes. And there's no medical pay for that kind of damage."

Later, when Irene had gone, and his little brothers were outside playing with neighbors, Trino found his mother looking at the newspaper that Irene had left behind. He noticed her finger sliding down the columns of the *Help Wanted* page.

When she saw Trino watching her, she frowned. "Are you going to work for Mr. Epifaño anymore? We need some money, not just his dented cans."

"Mom, I'm just a kid. Nobody's going to pay a kid for a real job." Trino was tired, tired from his work today, tired of his mother making them live this way. "Why can't you find a job?"

"You don't think I'm looking?" she said, her dark eyes shining with anger.

"I think you should go over to the college and see about that job that Nick was talking about—just like Tía Reenie said." He added the part about Tía Reenie since his mom liked her so much.

"You think I can just walk up to some lady at a desk and tell her I need a job and she'll give it to me, just like that?" She snapped her fingers to emphasize her words.

"I don't know why you can't try," Trino replied. "I was scared when I had to ask this librarian to show me how to use the computer at school. I thought she would just yell at me because Zipper and I used to cause trouble. But she wasn't mean to me. She showed me how to do some stuff so I could use a computer like the other kids do."

"This isn't a junior high school, Trino. I'm going to a college. You think I fit in there?"

Despite the angry glare in her eyes, Trino gave her a little grin. "You think I fit in at a college? I'm supposed to meet a few kids from school at the college library tomorrow afternoon so we can do that history project. How do you think we all feel? A bunch of seventh-graders working in a college library."

"Why do you have to go there? Just ride the bus to the city library."

"The college library has books written by *latinos*. Coach Treviño told us that if we looked for books written by *latinos*, we'd get more information about the *tejanos*."

His mother continued staring at Trino, but the fire had gone out of her eyes. He seemed to feel less angry, too. He knew he had to help his mother if he could, anyway he could.

"Listen, Mom, tomorrow when I'm over at the college, I'll look around a little. I can tell you what it's like. My friend, Lisana, told me that Bus 75 leaves you right in front of the college. It should be easy to find the library, don't you think?"

She shrugged, then lowered her eyes back to the newspaper. "Go see what your brothers are doing. I'm busy right now," she said, and her voice sounded very sad.

Trino had a different understanding of his mother's nervousness about a college campus as he stepped off the bus. Behind a large brick wall with the college name formed in broad, white letters were tall brick buildings. They sat among connecting parking lots, sidewalks, and green areas covered with shady trees. It seemed like a big complex that stretched out as far as he could see. Only a handful of people walked around on this Sunday afternoon.

He thought about hanging out at the bus stop and waiting for the others, but he didn't know what time it was. There would be a clock inside a library—if he could figure out which building it was. He decided to follow a trio of girls who were walking towards a tall white building with narrow windows. They turned and giggled at him before they went inside. He stopped and looked around, and finally saw the sign, *Semel Hall*. Even though he didn't know what *Semel Hall* could be, he knew it wasn't a library. He turned around and spotted a round building with rows of steps in front of it. When he saw a sign with an arrow *Academic Library*, he felt like he had found a dollar.

Through heavy glass doors, Trino walked into the building. He was surprised by the colorful artwork hanging from the ceiling. There were blue sofas near the tall windows and big comfortable green chairs, like a room in somebody's house. A few students stood near gray metal machines, talking as they put in coins and made copies. Trino noticed all the bookshelves, an aisle of computers down the middle of the room, and small study cubicles. He saw four tall tables with other computers set upon them. Against one wall, a long counter curved around like a snake, and behind it were more tables, bookshelves of videotape boxes, and two heavy desks, like the ones teachers used.

He walked up to one of the computers on a tall table and stared at the screen.

"What'cha looking for?" said a friendly voice behind him.

Trino had jumped a little before he turned around. It was a thin girl with long black hair. She wore glasses that had pink lenses in them. Her clothes were normal, just jeans and a T-shirt. She looked older—a college student, Trino guessed. But she was smiling at him, so he answered her.

"I'm trying to find some books about this man. It's for a school project."

"Of course it's for school. Why else does anybody come into a library on a Sunday? So, do you know how to use this machine?" She stepped sideways and placed her hand on the keyboard. When Trino shrugged, she gave a soft laugh. "It's a cinch, really. There are directions at the bottom of each screen. Just select what you're looking for and punch in a number. Good luck!" She walked away towards the bookshelves.

Trino read the screen slowly. *1. Title Keyword 2. Subject Keyword 3. Author. Enter your selection and press ENTER.*

Chewing on his bottom lip as he concentrated, Trino pressed **2** then **ENTER**. The screen went blank, then a long yellow box appeared. The instructions below it told him to type in the subject in the box and gave an example. Trino opened his notebook to be sure he spelled everything right: *navarro, jose antonio.*

When he saw two titles appear on the screen, he whispered to himself, "All right! I think I can do this."

At the bottom of the screen were more directions to get information about each of the books. He followed other directions, and returned to the original screen. He pushed the **2** button again, and this time typed *Texas Revolution* inside the yellow box.

By the time that Lisana, Jimmy, Hector, and Amanda showed up, Trino had written down the titles and numbers for six books on José Antonio Navarro and the Texas Revolution. He wrote down the floors where the books could be found, even if he didn't know where the elevator was located.

"I decided that you can *find* the books," he told them. "I shouldn't have to do all the work by myself."

Chapter Ten

Words and Deeds

None of them expected it would be so difficult to *read* the books they found. Even Amanda, who Lisana said was *real* smart, kept scratching her head and making faces as she flipped through the pages.

The five of them sat at a long table on the fourth floor, each one looking for information from a different book. The college library was very quiet. Only a handful of college students sat at the tables or walked through the bookshelves.

From the start, Trino had enjoyed the silence of the large room. It was so different from the busy noise of school or the crowded commotion at his house. He thought about his mom, working in a place like this. He bet she'd enjoy the quiet, too.

"Look at this," Hector grumbled, giving Trino's arm a nudge. "There are no pictures in this book. Just pages and pages of writing—and the print is so small. How are we supposed to read a book like this in one afternoon?"

"We don't have to read the whole book," Lisana told him. "We just take notes on the information we find. Then we put it into our own words for the report."

Jimmy held a thick green book about the Texas Revolution, but he hadn't opened it yet. "How long does the report have to be?" he asked.

"Coach said about four pages," Amanda said, then sighed. "I guess he figured that each partner could write two pages."

"I never wrote two pages about anything," Trino said out loud.

Everyone looked at Trino with surprised expressions.

He knew he could be honest with Lisana, but it was time to see if the others would accept him like he was. He stared at them one by one as he said, "Well, it's true. I'm not big on school stuff like you guys."

"They're the ones big on school stuff." Jimmy gestured with a thumb towards his sister. "Only *my* sister would use college books for a seventh-grade report. And when Coach paired Lisana up with Amanda, I thought, 'Well, there's a pair of *A* reports right there.' These two are going to make the rest of us look bad."

"Maybe Coach put us together because he knew we would be good *partners*. One of us wouldn't do all the work because the other one is lazy," Lisana said, then stuck her tongue out at Jimmy.

"I'm not lazy," Jimmy replied. "See?" He finally opened the green book to the back and started going over the index. "I'll look for the pages that mention Burnet, write down some notes, and call Mario tonight to read to him what I found. Happy?"

Amanda looked up from the book and said, "You know, Lisana, what's making this so hard is that I don't know what to put in the middle. Of course, Coach wants us to tell when Francisco Ruiz lived and died, but gosh—

we've got a whole lifetime here. What do we put down and what do we leave out?"

"Didn't Coach make you write down ten questions?" Trino asked Amanda.

"Ten questions?" She gave him a long-eyed look, as if Trino shouldn't even talk to her.

Trino spoke to Lisana instead, "Coach told Hector and me to write down ten questions about Navarro. He told us that if we answered all our questions, the report would fall right into our hands." He left out the part about getting in trouble.

"What kind of questions?" Lisana asked him, leaning slightly across the table.

Trino opened up his spiral notebook. He was embarrassed that it looked so crumpled and torn. He knew that Amanda thought he was a loser. Every time she had to speak to him she looked like she had a stomachache.

He found the page where he had written all his questions. He was glad that he had already written down some answers below them. "You told me that Navarro was one of the *tejanos* who signed the declaration, so I started there. Then I thought of other questions about him—my mom gave me some ideas too."

He could see Lisana was reading what he had written down. "This is a good idea, Trino." She picked up the notebook and showed it to Amanda. "Look, Amanda, we could do the same thing. We could follow Trino's questions for Franscico Ruiz."

"Not for everything," Trino said. "Ruiz was Navarro's uncle. Since he was older, he probably spent more time in Mexico than Texas."

Lisana smiled. "How did you know that Ruiz and Navarro were related? I almost told you the other day, but I didn't."

"It didn't surprise me when I found out. I figured if they were the only *tejanos* to sign the Texas declaration, there had to be a deeper connection. *Familia*. It made sense." Trino gave Amanda his own long-eyed look. "Amanda, you'd need to be *tejano* like Lisana and me to get it."

"I grew up in Texas, Trino. I know what *familia* means." Amanda's manner was as smooth as her voice. "Ruiz and Navarro loved Texas and wanted it to be independent. Just like my relatives who settled here."

"Amanda's mom traced her family heritage," Lisana said. "Did you know that her relatives were part of Stephen F. Austin's first colony? Isn't that cool?"

"Cool," Trino said, because he didn't know what else to say. He had wanted to be mean to Amanda because of the way she looked at him, but he was the one who felt embarrassed. Amanda had famous relatives. Maybe that's why she thought she was better than him.

Lisana pointed to something on Trino's notebook. "Wow, Amanda. Look at this last question of Trino's. *What happened after Navarro signed the declaration?* If we could find the answer to that question for Ruiz, wouldn't it make a great ending paragraph?"

"Hey, wait a minute!" Hector said, suddenly pulling the notebook out of Lisana's hand.

"These are our questions. You can't copy us."

"We don't need your dumb old questions," Amanda said, giving Hector one of those "you're just a cockroach" looks she gave so well. "Lisana and I can figure things out on our own."

Lisana lowered her eyes to the reference book in front of her. She drummed her fingers on the table. Amanda, Jimmy, Hector, and Trino seemed to follow her lead and began to read the books in front of them

The book Trino had been trying to read wasn't a regular book. It was called a "thesis." Amanda had told them that a "thesis" was a project for a graduate student—that her father did two of them to get his science degrees. She had told them that really good thesis projects were made into books. Her father's was at his university in Austin in its library.

Trino felt very dumb as he tried to read something written by an advanced college student. He skipped a few pages, then would try to read again, but it still seemed hard to understand. He skipped a larger group of pages and looked down again. A line of Spanish caught his attention. "*El tiempo hablará por todo.*" *Time will speak for everything.* It was in quotation marks. Did Navarro say this?

Trino started reading the paragraphs above and below the Spanish sentence. He shifted in his chair and eagerly turned a page. He had found the section about the Texas Declaration of Independence. After reading and re-reading, Trino understood that after Navarro signed the paper, he said, "*El tiempo hablará por todo.*" It never occurred to Trino that Navarro spoke Spanish, but it made sense. What guts it must have taken for Navarro and his uncle to walk into a room of fifty men who didn't speak the same language as they did!

Trino took his notebook back from Hector.

"Did you find something?" Hector asked, then yawned. He had leaned his head into his arm as he read from the book in front of him.

"I think I did. I'm just not sure what to do with it." Trino took the nearest pen and started writing, *El tiempo hablará por todo.*

"What does that mean?" Hector asked, leaning closer to Trino.

"Don't you speak Spanish?"

"Not much. What does that sentence mean?"

"*El tiempo hablará por todo.* It means 'Time will speak for everything.' According to this book, that's what Navarro said after he signed the Texas Declaration of Independence," Trino told Hector.

"Does your book say anything about Francisco Ruiz?" Amanda asked with an anxious voice. "Did Ruiz say anything after *he* signed the declaration?"

Trino looked back, tracing some sentences with his fingers. He looked up and shrugged. "There's nothing about Ruiz on this page." He saw Amanda's eyes dull with disappointment. Since she was Lisana's friend, he said. "When I'm finished, you can use this book, Amanda. I bet you'll find something since you probably read faster than I do."

"Thanks — Trino." Amanda gave him a little smile.

"*El tiempo hablará por todo.* It's almost like a line of a poem," Lisana said.

Both Jimmy and Hector rolled their eyes as they said, "Aw, man — not poetry."

Waving off the boys' reaction, Lisana said to Trino, "Navarro's words are really important. Could Amanda and I use them, too? I mean, we'll tell everyone that Navarro said it — and I promise that we'll tell Coach that *you* found the sentence in a book. When you think about it — that time will speak for everything — I mean — it's so truthful. Sometimes when you're first doing something, you just don't know if it'll work out. But Navarro signed the paper and truly believed that everything would work out well for the Texans. And it did."

"I think it's cool that Navarro and Ruiz, two *tejanos* that probably didn't speak English, come into this room filled with Anglos—" He looked at Amanda, and suddenly slowed his words, "—and they all work together because they all want the same thing."

Trino nodded, feeling very proud of what he had learned today. *El tiempo hablará por todo.* He looked at Hector. "Should we let Lisana and Amanda use the words I found?"

Hector chewed on his bottom lip a moment, then said, "I guess we can. Since Ruiz is related and everything. 'Course they can bring us some brownies or cookies on Monday as payment. After all, we found such a—" He paused to change his voice, "—bee-you-tee-full line of poetry!"

Everyone laughed together at Hector's silly voice, then Lisana copied down Navarro's words into her notebook. Then she wrote *Trino* to the side of the Spanish words and drew a smiling face inside the **o.**

〜 〜 〜

Irene and Trino's mom had made cookies with a jar of the apricot jelly and the torn bag of flour that Trino had brought home from Mr. Epifaño's store. The house smelled good, even though it was hotter than usual because the oven had been on.

Tía Reenie kept calling Trino "college boy," but Trino didn't mind because he had come home from the college feeling like a different person. He and Hector had more facts for their report, and he was starting to get excited about telling the class what he had learned about José Antonio Navarro, a real *tejano* hero. Amanda had started to act nicer, and he still felt really special that Lisana had written his name in her notebook.

But the best part had come when Jimmy had teased Trino in the library.

"Trino, your handwriting looks like a chicken scratched it out."

Trino had glanced at Jimmy's notebook and said, "Well, at least I know that freedom has two e's in it."

Later as they walked back to the bus stop, Hector had said, "Hey, Trino, trying to start a new style with those holes in your shoes?"

And once again, Trino managed to come back with a friendly put-down. "I'm just glad that my feet aren't as big as yours, Hector. My whole family could live in your shoes."

The joking around had made Trino feel like he was welcomed into their group.

Now that he was home, he enjoyed the jelly cookies his mom and her *comadre* had baked. Working in the library had made him very hungry.

"So what is the college like?" his mother asked, sitting down by Trino at the kitchen table. "Did you look around?"

"It's pretty big, Mom. There are *a lot* of buildings. I can see why they need more help cleaning all those rooms. I only saw the library inside. It's so quiet in there. And they keep it so clean. They have a lot of computers and books, of course," Trino said.

"So does my godson think he's going to go to college?" Tía Reenie asked. She stood at the oven, checking on the tray of cookies still baking. "Going to be a school boy now?"

Trino didn't have to answer because Beto came inside crying. He had scraped his knee. Félix returned home a little later from his weekend with his father. The man had sent only a twenty-dollar bill for their mother.

Irene and his mother started talking about men who cheat their kids out of child support money and other stuff that Trino didn't want to hear about. He grabbed two jelly cookies and went into his bedroom to read again what he had written down about Navarro. Imagining the past would be more fun than living in his present.

~ ~ ~

"What are you two up to? I haven't seen you leave this table the entire period." Coach Treviño stood behind the table where Trino and Hector had been copying their notes and turning them into a report.

"We're writing the report," Hector said. "This is the only time we can do it. I've got practice and Trino works after school." He didn't stop writing even as he spoke to his teacher.

"Trino, you work?" Coach asked him.

Trino put down his pen. His hand hurt from all the writing he had done in the past hour. He looked over his shoulder at Coach. "Just a couple of hours every day helping out a man in a store. His arm is broken."

Coach Treviño smiled at Trino. "It probably doesn't pay much, but I bet you feel good helping him."

The job softened Trino's guilty feelings because he didn't help Mr. Epifaño when Rosca had beat him up. A little pocket money wasn't bad either. Trino shrugged off Coach's comment and picked up his pen again.

"*El tiempo hablará por todo*. Where did you find those words?" Coach's voice sounded deep with suspicion.

Trino's hand shook a little as he said, "In a book about Navarro."

"In our library?"

"We went to the university library on Sunday, Coach," Hector said, his voice ringing with pride. "Trino found those words in a thee—uh? What did Amanda call it?"

"A thesis," Trino answered. He lifted his head, also feeling proud about what they had done on Sunday. He turned and looked at Coach Treviño. "A graduate student did his thesis on Navarro, and I read some of it. After Navarro signed the paper, this is what he said." He almost laughed at the raised eyebrows and open-mouth expression on his teacher's face.

"I'm impressed, guys. *Really* impressed that you both went out to the college library to get this information. You two are going to teach the class a lot when you give your report."

"Will you give us extra credit since we used college books?" Hector asked, turning himself in his chair.

Coach Treviño chuckled, clapping one hand down on Trino's and Hector's shoulders.

"Guys, I'll give you all the extra credit you want, any time you want. You just need to do the work."

As their teacher walked away, Trino and Hector turned towards each other.

"All right!" they both said, and put their hands together in a high-five.

❧ ❧ ❧

Friday after school, it wasn't Mr. Epifaño who stood at the cash register. It was a younger man with a bushy moustache and big rabbit teeth. Trino knew it was Mr. Epifaño's son. He had taken his father's place for a short time after Mr. Epifaño had been hurt by Rosca.

"You must be the boy who helps my old man. Well, he won't need you anymore." His voice was rough and mean. "He's at the clinic getting his cast off. I got to pick him up later. I'll just close down the store for an hour. What else can I do?"

In the past few weeks, Trino had met several of Mr. Epifaño's male relatives. Not one of them seemed to actually care about the old man. Mr. Epifaño worked hard in his store. Trino had seen it. And he was fair with his customers, even offering a little credit to people who were short on money. And after the first few days, Trino didn't have to beg for his pay. Mr. Epifaño gave it to Trino before he left, and had even started giving him two nice dollars, not crummy bills or a handful of change.

"I can stay and watch the store," Trino told Mr. Epifaño's son. "If you show me how to work the cash—"

"You think I'm going to leave a punk like you in the store while I'm gone?" The man spit something brown onto the floor, a floor that Trino had mopped faithfully every day for the past month. "You think I'll trust you with the cash register, boy? How stupid is that? Now, get out of here. No telling what you've been up to in this store the past few weeks!"

Trino's body stiffened as his fists curled up at his side. He wanted to leap over the counter and punch his fist right into those rabbit teeth and break out every one of them.

Suddenly he remembered that look on Nick's face when Mr. Caballero had tried to cheat him out of their tree money. He understood Nick's rage, because, like Nick, Trino had worked hard for the job he was paid to do. Now this man, Mr. Epifaño's son, was saying that Trino's work didn't deserve any kind of praise—that after all this time, Trino couldn't be trusted to watch the store for an hour while the son went to bring his father back from the clinic?

Trino wasn't going to let Mr. Epifaño's son cheat him out of a job. Even if Mr. Epifaño's arm was out of a cast, it didn't mean the man couldn't use some help at this store. And help wasn't going to come from his son or nephew, that's for sure.

He used all the strength of his anger to his advantage as he spoke to Mr. Epifaño's son. "Tell Mr. Epifaño I will come back tomorrow." Trino's voice was clear and deadly serious. "Mr. Epifaño and I can talk about my job. You don't have a say about it."

The guy with the big teeth snarled at him like a mad *javalina*.

Trino turned on his heel and walked out of the store like a man who had better places to go.

Chapter Eleven
Changes in the Wind

As Trino walked home from Mr. Epifaño's store, he felt the changes around him. Not just the thought of losing his job and extra spending money, but something in the weather, too. What had been a sticky day was turning cooler. He could smell rain in the breeze that rustled the tree branches along the street. He never paid much attention to the seasons, until they forced him to hope his mom could find a cheap, but warm jacket at a thrift store. It could be a bad winter for all of them if his mother didn't find a job.

Trino came home to a locked door. He looked around to be sure no one watched him. Then he lifted the trash can and took out the key his mother left under there whenever she worked late. As he opened the door, he wondered where she was, and where his brothers were.

He saw the note on the table, scribbled on a torn sheet of notebook paper.

> I go to coleg for a job
> Get boys at Mala hows

She had gone to the college after all. He felt relieved, especially since his job with Mr. Epifaño would probably end soon. He was surprised she hadn't said anything about going to the college this week. Of course, Trino had been too busy. If he wasn't working after school for Mr. Epifaño, he was reading over his history report or recopying it in his best handwriting. But as he stopped to think about it, he realized that she *had* seemed extra quiet the last few days.

He felt the first drops of rain as he walked the short distance to Mala's house, a small duplex across an empty lot behind the trailer park. The old woman had been taking care of Gus and Beto while their mother worked since Trino's family had moved into the neighborhood.

"I fed the boys a can of soup, so your *mamá* doesn't have to rush with supper," Mala told Trino as she pushed Gus and Beto out the door. "I gotta go. My *telenovela* just started."

It took him longer to walk home because Gus and Beto kept stopping and staring up at the drizzle that fell upon them.

"Rain, rain, come and play. Rain, rain, go away." Beto sang his words as he stomped his feet into the dry grass.

"Wet head," Gus said, patting his black hair with his hand. He stopped to look up and then waved his hand in front of his eyes when the rain fell in them. "Wet, wet. I'm wet."

"Come on, guys! It's gonna start pouring, and you two walk too slow," he said.

He finally picked up Gus and carried him. They had to get home before the dark skies around them burst open with heavy rain.

By the time Trino got Beto and Gus back to the trailer, Félix's bus had just dropped him off. Steady rain began just as Trino unlocked the door and let his brothers inside.

"We lucked out, man," Félix said as Trino went to the refrigerator to look for something to eat. "The rain's really coming down now."

He knew they had truly "lucked out" when he saw the packages of lunch meat and sliced cheese on the middle shelf. There were two loaves of bread on the counter and a package of cookies, the white creme kind that they all loved, but were just too expensive to buy.

For a second Trino wondered, *Did I walk into the wrong trailer?*

Trino and Félix made themselves two sandwiches each. Trino wanted to drink the last dented soda can, but he didn't want to share it four ways. He hid it behind the mustard jar, and hoped he could sneak it out later. When his brothers wanted to eat cookies, Trino gave Félix, Beto, Gus, and himself only three cookies apiece.

"We can't eat the whole package today," Trino said when Gus and Beto asked for two more cookies. "We got to save some for tomorrow."

Suddenly, he realized he sounded like his mother. *Too weird*, he thought.

Things got boring. They were stuck inside together because of the rain, and their television set was still broken. Gus and Beto started whining like cats. They wanted more cookies; they wanted to go back to Mala's house and watch her TV. They wanted to go outside and play in the rain.

"You can't go outside. Stop bugging me. It's not my fault it's raining. Go find something to do," Trino said in a grouchy way. He was lying on the sofa, trying to fall asleep, despite his brothers' noise and the steady sounds of the rain on the trailer house roof.

A loud crack of thunder sent the two little boys squealing. They both jumped on top of Trino.

"Hey!" Trino yelled as Beto's bony knees jabbed into his stomach at the same time Gus body-slammed his legs.

He nearly fell off the sofa as he tried to get up and throw his brothers off of him.

There was another burst of thunder before Félix yelled, "Dog pile!" and jumped on top of the squirming bodies on the sofa. Trino groaned at the sudden extra weight. He grabbed whatever brother or limbs that he could. Everybody pulled arms and pushed legs. Soon they were a bundle of arms and legs, laughing and screeching. They rolled off the sofa like a tangle of webworms and wrestled together on the worn red carpet.

"Hey! No biting!" Trino yelled when he felt little teeth on his wrist.

But he had to laugh at Beto's squinted eyes and gritted teeth as the little boy tried to push himself out of Félix's head lock. Trino tried to flip Félix over to help Beto out.

Suddenly, the door to the trailer house flew open, and the damp wind made everyone let go and scramble away.

Trino saw his mother first. Her soaked clothes and wet, stringy hair dripped water all over the doorway, but it didn't matter because rain coming through the open door had soaked the carpet quickly. She struggled against the wind to get the door closed, and Trino jumped up to help her.

"*Ay, ay, ay,* look at all this water! Go get some towels. Get *me* a towel!"

Another loud burst of thunder made Beto and Gus squeal again, especially when the lights started to flicker. They ran towards their mother, but she pushed them away. Her wet hands slid over the boys, but she kept them as far away from her body as she could.

"Get away from me! I'm soaking wet." She kicked off her black shoes by the door. "I've ruined my good shoes for sure. And look at this dress—it's only good for rags now. Félix! Don't just stand there with your mouth open. Take care of your brothers so I can change out of these clothes. And get some towels for the floor—did you hear me?" She walked across the carpet, her stocking feet squishing with every step.

Trino knew that their thin towels wouldn't help dry the carpet much, but he and Félix put them down anyway as their mother changed. Beto and Gus laughed as they stomped on the towels and got their feet wet.

As the lights flickered again, Trino looked out the small front window. He could barely see the rain since it had grown darker. But he could hear it pelting the roof like falling stones. The wind whistled through the trailer park, making Trino glad he was inside watching and not outside walking.

"Let me see, Trino," Beto said, pulling on his big brother's T-shirt. "I want to see the rain."

"There's nothing to see. It's too dark." He dropped the thin curtain and looked down at Beto.

"Can we fight some more? That was fun." The little boy smiled at Trino.

"Maybe later." He noticed the lights flicker again. "I need to find some candles and matches just in case the lights go out. Félix, you still got that flashlight that Oscar gave you?"

"Yeah, what about it?"

"If the lights go out, we'll need it. Go find it."

"It's my flashlight. Nobody else can use it but me," he answered, then left the living room with Beto and Gus trailing after him.

"I haven't seen it rain like this in years," Trino's mom said as she came back into the room. She wore faded blue sweatpants and a T-shirt, and was still towel-drying her long black hair. "And of course it got worse when I got off the bus to walk home. At least I didn't have to talk to Mr. Escobedo looking like a drowned cat."

"Who's Mr. Escobedo?" Trino asked.

"He's in charge of Housekeeping at the college. He's very nice." She laid the damp towel over the back of a kitchen chair and walked towards the refrigerator. "I hope you boys left me something to make a sandwich with. Did you eat up all the cookies?"

"Where did the food come from?" Trino asked her. "Did Nick come over or something?" Lately, when they ate well, it was because of him.

"I bought the food. I had a little left over after I gave Mrs. Cummins the rent money." She gave Trino a crooked smile. "I just couldn't eat any more eggs, you know?"

Trino nodded. He had been thinking the same thing for weeks.

She opened up the refrigerator door. As she pulled out the package of sandwich meat, a loud crash of thunder made the trailer shake.

Beto and Gus squealed loudly from the bedroom, then came running towards their mother. "Mamá! Mamá!" they cried over and over again.

Beto tried to scramble up his mother's body as Gus hugged her legs tightly.

The lights flickered again, then completely went out. Both little boys start to cry loudly. A dim stream of light came from the direction of the bedrooms.

"I found this just in time." Félix's voice came from behind the beam.

"It won't last long," Trino said. "The batteries must be old."

"*Cálmense, niños.*" Their mother's gentle voice seemed strangely out of place. "Don't be scared. We're all together. We're safe and dry. Félix, go to my bedroom. Bring me the two *veladoras* on the back shelf. We'll light the holy candles to bring us light, and to thank *La Virgen* that your *mamá* found a job today."

Despite the darkness around him, despite his little brothers' crying and the sounds of a storm raging around them, Trino felt lighthearted.

He took a step forward and bumped his leg into a kitchen chair. "Ouch!" A flash of lightning came through the small windows in the trailer, giving a thin outline to his mother's body hunched over to hug the two frightened boys beside her.

"Hey, Félix, hurry up with the candles!" Trino yelled. He put his hands out, feeling for the other chairs, and the edge of the table. His knee hit another chair leg before he managed to get around the table. He used the sounds of his brothers' crying to guide his steps.

He felt his mother's back, and gently patted it. "I'm glad you got the job, Mom," he said.

Following her arms, he found one of two little shaking bodies. He thought about his friend, Hector, trembling in the janitor's closet, and remembered what he did to help Hector stay calm. He also remembered the way Hector did funny voices to make them laugh.

"Hey, whose body is this?" Trino said in a squeaky voice. "Who is this?" He felt Beto's soft hair and gave it a little pull. "What is this? Is this a little dog? I can't tell in the dark."

"It's me — Beto," said an unsteady little voice. "I'm not a dog."

"Are you a horse?"

Beto's voice grew stronger. "I'm not a horse. I'm a boy."

Trino got his hands around Beto's body and firmly pulled him from his mother's arms. "I just can't tell in the dark. Let me hold you so I can feel that you're a little boy. Let's see. I feel two skinny arms. Oh, and there's two skinny legs. Is there a tail? No, no tail. Okay, I guess you're a little boy named Beto." Trino tickled Beto and poked him. Wrapping one arm across Beto's chest, he reached out to Gus. "And you? Are you a horse?" As quickly as they had started crying, both boys began to laugh.

"I found the candles," Félix said as the dim beam of light reappeared in the room. "Do we have any matches?"

In a minute, two candles burned on the table. Like moths, both little boys came to the light. Beto climbed onto the chair, and Gus climbed up to sit on the table.

"Lights!" Gus said, pointing a small hand towards the kitchen walls.

One of the holy candles had a colorful image of *La Virgen de Guadalupe* painted on the tall glass. The flame made red, green, and yellow spots flicker on the walls. The other candle had diamonds of blue, yellow, white, and purple on it, like a colorful window at a church.

"We should tell ghost stories," Félix said, and put the flashlight under his chin. The light made his chin, lips, and nose look as if they glowed. His voice deepened. "I could tell you the story of three boys who went into a cave and turned into goats."

Trino stood behind Beto's chair. "Were the goats' names Félix, Nacho, and Frank?"

"Shut up," Félix said, and then cleared his throat. His voice deepened again. "The story begins on a stormy night—just—like—this—one. Three boys went in search of

this secret cave where evil spirits make noises like screaming women. They said the devil lived in this — ow!"

Félix's head jerked forward, like he had just gotten a
knock in the head.

"What's wrong with you?" Their mother's sharp voice
sounded even madder in the darkness. "Telling a story
about evil spirits with *veladoras* burning on our table. If
you're going to tell a story to your brothers, make it a story
that has some goodness in it."

"That's no fun," Félix said, lowering the flashlight.

"We don't need evil spirits in this house. Even though
the storm's bad, a good thing happened today. I got a job.
I don't want your talk of the devil to bring us bad luck,"
she said, shaking a finger at Félix.

Their mom sat down to eat a sandwich, only to give
half of it to Gus and Beto. They asked for more cookies,
and their mom put the package on the table and divided
the rest among them. The two extras, she ate herself.

Félix made shadow animals on the wall until the flashlight beam went out. They all sat in the silence of the burning candles. No cookies to eat, no flashlight to play with,
no ghost stories to tell.

A loud burst of thunder shook the trailer again. Gus
climbed into his mother's lap. Beto put his arms around
her shoulders.

"I wish Nick was here," Félix said. "He could tell us a
funny story or something."

"Well, he's not here, so think of something else," his
mom said, then suddenly stood up, pushing poor Beto
away, and setting Gus on the floor. "You two let me go. I
got to go to the bathroom."

She didn't even take a candle with her, she just stomped
into the darkness.

Gus and Beto moved over towards Trino's chair. Their eyes were round with fear.

Trino found himself wishing that Nick was with them, too. Not for a funny story, but for someone to talk to. There was so much Trino could tell him: about Mr. Epifaño, about his new friends, about his school project.

That's when Trino raised his head and looked at Beto and Gus. "I could tell you a story about a man I learned about. It won't be a funny story like Nick tells, but I thought his life was pretty interesting. His name was José Antonio—"

Bam! Something hard and heavy landed on top of the trailer. The force knocked the candles over. One went out, as the other rolled down the table. Trino caught the candle before it fell off. He stared at the image of *La Virgen* for only a second before he heard his mother's screaming.

"Trino! Félix! Help me!"

But Trino couldn't move. Beto and Gus had screamed for their mother, and clamped their arms around Trino. They jumped on his feet, pulling at his clothes. He heard weird metallic sounds. Was something bending or breaking above them?

"Félix, we got to get out of here," he said, peeling Beto off of his legs and pushing him towards Félix. "I think whatever fell on the trailer might come through the roof."

Félix's body shook like crazy, his black eyes were wide open and filling with tears.

"Félix, you gotta take Beto and Gus. Get out of here. I got to help Mom." When Félix didn't move to take Beto or Gus, Trino screamed, "Félix! Get the kids out of here!"

Trino grabbed Gus and lifted him into Félix's arms. Beto screamed and kicked, but Félix managed to drag him by one arm towards the door. A wet burst of wind hit all of them. The last candle on the table blew out. All the boys screamed louder, but Trino couldn't help them. He had to find his mother.

His only consolation was that she was still screaming out Trino's name. He tripped on something, fell onto the sofa, then managed to stand up again. He stretched his arms in front of him as he walked. His hands hit the walls, then a metal fuse box on the wall, a light switch that didn't work. The hall had never seemed so long. Finally, he felt the door frame of the bathroom. As he stepped into it, a steady rain came at him from all sides.

"Mom!" he yelled. "Where are you?" He saw a large curved black thing above his head, but it was the spread of wet leaves and small branches that stopped him. "Mom!"

"Trino, I'm stuck. I can't get through."

He reached his hands through the leaves, ignoring the scratches and scrapes. "Mom! Mom! Can you find my hand?"

He tried not to let the darkness frustrate him, or the rain falling on his face keep him from getting to her. There were so many little branches in his way. Then he remembered the way that Nick had used his legs and feet to crack branches before they put them into the truck.

Trino stomped down on the branches, using his feet to break them, get them out of his way. The wet wood didn't break easily, but he didn't stop. His body was soaked by the time he caught sight of his mother's white T-shirt. She grabbed his hand, pushing herself through the branches as he pulled her forward. He heard her sounds of pain as the branches scratched her as much as they scratched him. But they both worked together stepping on branches, pushing away the leaves, and cracking sticks with their hands.

Finally, she stepped through the last of the tree branches. She was free.

"*Ay,* Trino—" She took a deep breath, and released it quickly. "*Gracias.*"

His hands still gripped her trembling ones. Then he realized he hadn't held his mom's hand in a long time.

Chapter Twelve
Man of Mud

"Where are the boys?" His mother released Trino's hands. "Are they safe?"

"I hope so. I—" He stopped talking when he heard the weird metallic noise again.

"We need to get out of here, Mom. Something doesn't sound right."

They both turned to face two small beams from a pair of flashlights.

"Trino? María? Are you okay?" A man's voice came from beyond the flashlights.

"Who is it?" Trino said, wishing he could see better.

"It's Mr. Cummins. The boys came over to our trailer. They said you needed help," he answered.

As their landlord stepped closer, Trino could finally see the short, heavy man. His black skin and dark clothes made him seem almost invisible, but his eyes revealed his genuine concern for them.

"Are my boys okay?"

"Sure." His white teeth appeared in a smile. "Mrs. Cummins was drying them off and trying to find some dry clothes in the dark when I left to find you. The whole trailer park lost its power."

The two flashlight beams shone into the bathroom. Trino could see the branches better now, and all the broken sticks and torn leaves all over the floor.

Mr. Cummins gave a loud whistle. "What a mess! You're lucky to be alive, María."

"My mom's had luck with her all day," Trino said, feeling relieved someone else was there to help them. He hadn't realized how scared he had been until now, when he stopped to think about it.

The weird metallic sounds groaned above their heads. "What is that noise?" Trino asked Mr. Cummins.

"Sounds like the rest of the tree is on top of this trailer. We'd better get out of here just in case more comes through the roof. Come on!"

Trino's mom grabbed his hand again before they followed Mr. Cummins out of the trailer. She stopped only a moment to pick up the candles. "We might need these for extra light."

He was glad she had taken them. He didn't have much use for religious stuff, but with this storm, he figured it wouldn't hurt to keep two *veladoras* burning through the night.

⁓ ⁓ ⁓

The next morning, Trino knew he would never forget the sight. The large tree he had liked to climb now had a jagged split from top to trunk. Most of the bushy branches fell on their trailer, covering it with a wig of leaves and sticks. One large branch looked like a giant elbow leaned into the top of the trailer. It was the same branch that had come through the ceiling just as their mother had stepped into the bathtub to look out the bathroom window.

"Yesterday, I thought things were finally going to change." His mother's words dripped with bitterness. "I got a job, finally! Today, I'm homeless. Why can't I get a lucky break just once in my life?"

Trino turned and recognized he had grown taller than his mother. He glanced back towards the trailer, then back at her. Had she been sitting on the toilet last night, instead of standing in the tub to look out the window, she might not be next to Trino right now, staring at what was left of their trailer house.

He had never talked much to his mother, but being around Hector and his new friends had made him feel more comfortable about saying what was on his mind.

"Mom, we don't got a house right now, but at least we've got all of us alive. I look at that—" he pointed towards the broken tree and smashed trailer. "—and I think, man, we lived through that. We're pretty lucky."

He saw her dark eyes fill with tears, before she started walking back towards the white trailer where the Cummins lived across the lot.

The Cummins were nice enough to share their floor with them last night, but then Mr. Cummins mentioned he had heard on his battery radio that there was an emergency shelter set up at the high school, and thought Trino's mom should go there for help. Trino knew their problems were getting worse by the minute.

Mr. Cummins wouldn't let them go back into the trailer to get any clothes. "My insurance man said to stay out of it—for safety's sake, you know," he said.

Their mother only had a thin pair of cloth slippers on her feet, Gus and Beto were barefoot, and all of them were wearing the only clothes they had left. As they walked out of the Cummins' trailer, Trino carried Beto while their mother carried Gus. Félix walked beside them, complaining, but no one answered him. Finally, he shut up and trudged along.

The trailer park lot was sloppy with muddy puddles and ditches of dirty water. Trino's clothes were stiff, and carrying Beto only made his steps heavier in the mud. Walking was hard and slow because he didn't want to slip and drop Beto.

Steady drizzle had started to fall as they walked in silence for six blocks to the high school. Whenever they reached sidewalks, Trino put Beto down to walk, but he had to carry him across areas with no walkways and streets where construction had just added to the sloppy mess in the neighborhood.

At the high school gym, his mother signed a couple of papers, and they went inside. Rows of cots were lined up around the gym floor with the middle space left empty for chairs and tables and an area where kids were playing board games.

Beto and Gus were anxious to join the other kids, and Trino was just glad to rest his arms after carrying Beto so long.

"Don't sit on the beds in those wet clothes," his mother said, so Trino and Félix ended up sitting on the bleachers near the cots their family had been assigned.

"This sucks," Félix said for the tenth time that day.

"Yeah, I know," Trino said, only he didn't know what was the worst thing: that he had no house, that he had no clothes, or that he had lost that feeling of "luck" he had felt earlier.

Lunch was hot dogs, chips, and cokes. The food was hot, and they could eat as much as they wanted. With food in his stomach and drier clothes, Trino started to feel as if he had come back to life. Only the life around him wasn't where he wanted to be.

Everyone had used the TV in the corner to catch up on the news. The storm had affected the whole city, knocking out electricity, flooding out some areas, and leaving behind fallen trees and other debris from the rising waters. Strangers in the gym started talking to one another, sharing their stories. Félix started talking to everyone about the tree falling on their house trailer, and he made it sound as if he had rescued their mom. It made Trino mad, but he was too tired to do anything about it. He just stretched out on the cot and tried to fall asleep.

Big excitement came an hour later when a lady with a microphone and a man with a video camera from a local television station came into the gym to interview people who had to leave their homes and come to this shelter.

"I want to be on TV," Félix said.

Trino still lay on a cot, his eyes closed. He could hear the babies crying, men talking loudly, and through it all, came a sad, long sigh he recognized as his mother's. He opened his eyes slightly, and saw that she sat on the cot beside his. Her face looked tired, as if she had just come home from working an extra shift or two. But there was something pathetic in the way her mouth was drawn down, the way her black hair hung limp around her shoulders.

"How long will we stay here, Mom?" he asked in a quiet voice.

"At least through tomorrow. I wish the phones worked. I think we might be able to stay with your Tía Sofia, or maybe Irene would put us up a few days. But if we leave the neighborhood, how will you boys get to school? Who will take care of Gus and Beto so I can start my new job?" She sighed again. "I'm so tired of all this."

"Why don't you try to sleep?" Trino leaned up on one elbow. He felt like he had to help his mother, but didn't know what to do, either. Maybe he could talk to someone and get some ideas.

"Excuse me, are you Trino?" said a female voice behind him.

He sat up on the cot and turned his head. A pretty woman in a clean red jacket and blue pants smiled at him. Her face had good make-up, and her hair was neat and combed. She just didn't fit in among the rained-out, messy people in the gym.

"Are you Trino?" she asked again, and that's when he saw the microphone in her hand. Behind her, stood a dark-haired man with a big video camera on one shoulder.

Suddenly, Beto bounced unto Trino's legs. "This is Trino. Ask him, lady."

"Get off me, Beto!" Trino said in a grouchy way, and pulled his brother off his legs. He swung himself around to stand up. Beto bounced on the empty cot and laughed.

"I understand from your little brother here that you rescued your mother last night when a tree fell on the trailer where you live. Is that true?" the woman asked him, holding the microphone a little closer to Trino's mouth.

He looked beyond the woman's shoulder and saw Félix standing there, but not for long. Félix moved around to stand beside Trino and be on TV, too.

Trino looked at the woman, then noticed a rubber camera lens moving closer to him.

"I—I just helped my mom, that's all," he said, feeling his legs turn cold. His stomach flip-flopped. Last night's feelings of desperation and fear seemed to be part of him again.

"I understand there was no electricity in your house. How did you find her?"

"I listened for her voice. I knew she was stuck in the bathroom."

The woman suddenly moved the microphone to Trino's left and said. "Is this your mother, Trino? Ma'am, how do you feel about your son's heroism? Are you proud of him—that he risked his own safety to save you?"

Trino's mother stood behind him. She stepped forward, moving her hair back from her face, trying to smooth it down with her fingers as she talked.

"My son Trino is a strong boy. I knew he could help me."

"But are you proud of him?"

"Of course I'm proud of him." Her voice showed her annoyance with the question. "I could have been stuck under that tree all night."

The woman put the microphone down and said, "That's good, Joe. We have enough at the shelter for now."

"Cool! Now we'll all be on TV." Félix grinned. "I've never seen myself on TV before."

"You'll look just as stupid on TV as you do in real life," Trino replied, only to get a shove in the shoulder from his little brother. Before Trino could hit him back, the news woman turned back towards them.

"Trino, would you mind taking a drive in our van? Could you take us to where you live?" she said. "I'd like to film your trailer house and show pictures of the tree on top of it."

~ ~ ~

When Mr. Cummins saw the white van with KVUE Channel 7 painted in red letters, he came out of his trailer to speak to the woman, who had told Trino to call her Liz, and to call the camera man, Joe. Before they could even unpack their equipment, he told them he *had* to show them worse damage from the storm in another part of the trailer park. Joe got the camera, and they looked eager to follow Mr. Cummins around.

"Wait here. We'll be right back," Liz told Trino.

Trino frowned, and leaned against the van. *What could be worse than a tree smashing your house?* he wondered as he watched Mr. Cummins lead them away. The man talked nonstop, making Trino glad he could stay behind.

Once again, he looked with amazement at the trailer. Someone had made a big X with yellow tape that had the word **DANGER** printed in black letters. Wondering what the inside of the trailer must look like, he stared at the door. Everything they owned, as little as it was, remained in that trailer. He hated the feeling of helplessness that had taken hold of him the past few hours. He looked at the broken tree, but found himself thinking about a way to cut it down, as if this whole nightmare was nothing more than a tree job he had with Nick.

And that's when Nick's words came back into Trino's head. *"Sometimes a man has to help himself before he can help others."*

A plan began to form in Trino's mind. He looked around for anyone watching him. He didn't see Mr. Cummins or the TV people anymore. But he knew the trailer park wasn't that big, and if he was going to act, he had to do it quickly. He looked around one more time, then ran to the front door. He yanked on the yellow tape. It pulled down easily.

The front door was stuck, but Trino leaned his shoulder into the door to get it open. Once inside, he could see wet towels that inches of mud, water, leaves, and sticks had jammed against the door. The floor was a squishy, sloshy mess. His shoes sank as he walked. Cold, dirty water slid through the holes in his tennis shoes. In four steps, his feet were soaked.

The trailer was dark, but there was some light coming through the small windows. He walked to the kitchen, hoping to find a trash bag in the cabinet by the refrigerator. He found two of them on a middle shelf, and said a quick "Yes!" Then he headed towards the bedroom.

The metallic sounds groaned above him. Trino looked up, wondering if the tree would eventually fall through the whole trailer. But if it did, Trino hoped it wouldn't be in the next two minutes.

Beto's and Gus's shoes floated near the sofa. They were soaked and caked with mud, but they could still be worn once they were cleaned up. He sloshed his way down the hall, and tried not to think about the mess in the bedroom he shared with his brothers. The smell was awful, like a pond where water never moved. Their beds were muddy, and the closet had filled with several inches of water. The clothes they had carelessly tossed on the floor were wet and dirty, so he didn't touch them. Instead he opened drawers and grabbed any clothes he found.

Then he went to his mother's room. He knew his mother needed shoes, and some kind of clothes she could wear to work. He saw her purse on top of the dresser and put it in the bag, too. The carpet squished under his feet as he walked around. He took pants from her closet, some blouses, and opened her drawers, too.

He felt weird grabbing his mother's underwear and bras, but he knew she'd need them, and stuffed them into the second bag. The metal noises above him sounded loudest in her bedroom, and Trino knew he had to hurry. As he worked, sweat slid down his back, and his throat felt like he had been walking in a desert.

Trino looked beside the bed, and felt a jolt of gladness. He found the black laced shoes his mom usually wore to work, as well as some worn-out sneakers she wore around the house. They were slimy with mud, but he grabbed a damp pillow, shook out the pillow, and put the shoes inside the pillowcase before he put them inside the trash bag, too.

He stopped only a moment to see the bathroom damage in the daylight, because the bags were getting heavy. He trudged along, thinking he must look like a barrio Santa Claus with the sacks slung over his shoulder.

When he got back to the front door, he realized that he had opened it just enough to get his body through. He pulled the door back with one hand as he held tight to the bags with the other. He didn't want to put the bags down and risk more mud and water getting into their clothes.

With clenched teeth and a second, more determined grip, he managed to get the door open wider, just enough to push the bags through and get his body out behind them.

"Trino! What do you think you're doing?"

Startled by the loud, angry voice, he nearly lost his footing on the doorstep. He caught himself by pushing against the sacks. He cushioned himself against the wall of the trailer house until he got his balance.

Trino came out of the trailer to face Mr. Cummins' pinched expression, the reporter's wide-open eyes, and the camera guy's amused grin.

"Are you crazy, boy? It's dangerous to be in there! What's wrong with you?" Mr. Cummins stomped towards Trino, pointing at the trailer as he talked. "I told your mom this morning that nobody could go in there. It's dangerous. The police even came to tape up the door. You could get arrested for going in there. Do you know that?"

Trino put the bags down. His arms felt numb from their weight, but at the same time, he felt very strong. He noticed Liz staring at him, and he remembered what the reporter had asked Trino's mom at the shelter. "Are you proud of him?"

This time Trino felt proud of himself. He stood up straight and faced Mr. Cummins' anger head on.

"Mr. Cummins, my family's got nothing right now," Trino said. "But my mom just got a new job, and she needs her clothes. My brothers have no shoes to wear, and this T-shirt and jeans is all I have left. If you had been me, wouldn't you have done the same thing to help your family?"

At that, Mr. Cummins' lips pressed together in a thick line across his face. His dark eyes still looked mad, but he didn't say anything else.

Trino turned around, and stepped back towards the trailer. With both hands, he pulled the door closed. He grabbed the tape and tried to press it back into place.

"That's okay, leave it. I'll fix it in a while myself," Mr. Cummins said. His voice seemed calmer. "I was going to get the extra key and lock the door anyway."

Trino nodded. "That's good, Mr. Cummins. We don't want anyone to take our stuff." Even if it was dangerous, he knew there were punks who would risk it just for a few things they could steal, even though Trino knew that nothing left inside was worth taking.

"Trino, why don't you load the sacks into our van, and we'll take you back to the shelter?" Liz told him, and he noticed she was blinking a lot. She took a deep breath, then stepped towards Mr. Cummins. "What are your plans for the trailer?" she asked him.

"I can't say right now. I'll have to get somebody out here to cut down the tree and get it off the trailer before I can see how bad the damage is," he answered.

Despite the weight in his arms, Trino turned back towards Mr. Cummins. "I know a man who cuts down trees. He and I work together on the weekends. He could — *we* could — do the job for you."

Mr. Cummins frowned as he shook his head. "No, I'm going to hire professionals. My insurance company will pay for someone good to do the job right. Sorry, kid."

His quick dismissal made Trino mad, but the loss of money, which his family needed so badly, made him even angrier.

As Trino walked to the KVUE van, his arms and legs ached. His shoes were filled with mud and water. He carried what was left of his family's clothes in two trash bags.

This should have been a grim scene in a TV movie, but here was Trino's life, mud and all.

Chapter Thirteen

Trino's Time

"Why didn't Trino get my new jeans and my RitzMaz T-shirt?" Félix complained as his mother sorted through the trash bags and separated their clothes onto their cots.

"If you didn't leave your clothes on the floor, then you'd have them," his mother said, snapping off the words. "Just be glad your brother brought you something else to wear. Now we all can take a shower and clean up."

Most of their stuff was damp, some of it dirty, but his mother smiled for the first time that day when she saw her purse and her clothes.

"I got into trouble with Mr. Cummins for going into the trailer, but I had to get our stuff," Trino told her.

"I should have done this myself," she answered, then started going through the bags. "I should have *made* him let us go inside our trailer."

That afternoon, everyone in his family got to take a shower, and put on damp, but clean clothes. Gus and Beto were entertained with the other small children by some older teens from a church group who played games with them. Félix met up with some boys from the school and hung out on the bleachers talking and looking at car magazines. Trino's mother got permission to use the football team's washer and dryer in the locker room to rinse out and dry their clothes. She made Trino stay with her, help her fold clothes, and stack them. They scrubbed the shoes clean, and set them on the bleachers to dry.

As they finished, some people showed up with sandwiches, baskets of oranges and apples, bottles of water, and boxes of cookies. Even though living in a gym was weird and boring, having food to eat when he was hungry made things bearable for Trino.

He had returned to the food table for another sandwich and more cookies, when he heard Félix calling his name. He turned in the direction of the TV since it was the last place where he had seen his brother.

"Trino! Quick! You're on TV!" Félix yelled so loud that others ran to the television set to watch.

Trino managed to elbow his way around two tall men, just in time to see Liz, the reporter, talking to him and his mom. They were the two people the camera focused on.

"*I understand there was no electricity in your house. How did you find her?*"

"*I listened for her voice. I knew she was stuck in the bathroom.*"

"*My son Trino is a strong boy.*" On TV, their mother looked like a teenager with her messy black hair and no make-up. "*I knew he could help me. I'm proud of him. I could have been stuck under that tree all night.*"

An image of Liz standing in front of the trailer appeared next.

Trino could hear the rumble of amazement in the voices of the people in the gym. Trino had to admit that on TV, the pictures of the tree on top of the trailer looked bad to him, too.

"But young Trino wasn't just a hero for his mother last night. Today Trino risked his life to go back into the trailer to get his family some clothes."

The cameraman, Joe, had taken video of Trino coming out of the trailer loaded down with two bulky black bags. Everyone watching TV heard Mr. Cummins yell, *"Trino! What do you think you're doing?"*

They saw Trino stumble, but push himself upright.

A close-up of Trino's face appeared next. It looked fatter than usual. His eyes were shiny black. His voice sounded deep like a man's. *"My family's got nothing right now. But my mom just got a new job, and she needs her clothes. My brothers have no shoes to wear, and this T-shirt and jeans is all I have left. If you had been me, wouldn't you have done the same thing?"*

The reporter then ended her piece by saying, *"Trino and his family have found shelter at Miller Park High School. For Trino's family and many others displaced by last night's terrible storm, this is the time to be grateful for what little you have, especially since there are others who have lost everything. This is Liz Medina, reporting for Channel 7, KVUE news."*

Everyone cheered as the final image of the people milling about inside the high school gym faded to black. A commercial for a pizza restaurant filled the screen. Those who lost interest in the television, walked away.

One of the men standing by Trino extended his hand. "Good job, son. You helped your family like a man should."

Trino shook the man's hand, just as he felt somebody touching his shoulder. He turned to see his mom smiling at him. He gave her a smile back. Then some of Félix's friends talked to Trino, asking him more about the tree hitting the trailer. Others who had watched the news came by their cots later to talk to Trino or his mom. He didn't know what to think about all the attention, but he was glad people smiled when they talked to him. He had been afraid people would think he was stupid for taking the chances that he did.

Later that night, when the gym lights were turned out, Trino finally had some time to think about the news report. Liz, the reporter, and Joe, the cameraman, had put words and pictures together that made Trino seem important. Some of the adults in the gym had used the word "hero." As Trino tried to get comfortable on the stiff cot, he wished that being a hero came with a money reward. His family needed a lot more than words of praise right now.

~ ~ ~

Since the next day was Sunday, a male preacher with a black shirt and white collar, two other ladies, and a pair of teenage girls came into the gym and asked everyone to join them in a prayer service. Trino was more interested in eating breakfast, but the people who were setting out boxes of cereal and little cartons of milk, announced that food came *after* prayers. Trino's mom made them all comb their hair with a comb someone had given them, and they had to stand together in the middle of the gym and listen to the preacher read from the Bible.

Trino watched the two girls standing by the preacher, thinking that the one with glasses looked familiar, somehow. Did she go to his school? She had a nice face, but the other girl had blonder hair, prettier blue eyes.

Later, after all the preacher's talking and praying were over, everyone got to eat some breakfast. Trino sat at a table, eating a third bowl of cereal when the girl in the glasses came up to stand by him.

"You go to Carson, don't you? I saw you on TV last night," she said.

Now that she was closer, the idea that Trino knew this girl seemed to press harder upon him. But he didn't want to sound dumb, just in case she just had one of those faces like everyone else. So he just nodded, saying nothing.

"I'm Stephanie. You're friends with Lisana and Jimmy, right?" She giggled, even though there was nothing to laugh at.

And then Trino remembered. "You're Amanda's friend." He also recalled that Amanda and Stephanie hadn't been very nice to him when they met at school. He made an effort to talk to her only because of Lisana. "Your dad's a preacher, huh?"

"Yeah. It was his idea to come here. This place smells bad, doesn't it?"

He wanted to tell her that a flooded trailer smelled even worse, but he heard a woman's voice call, "Stephanie! It's time to leave."

"Bye. Uh—see you at school, I guess."

As he watched Stephanie in her clean jeans and ironed pink blouse walk away from the table, he thought about Lisana and Jimmy, Hector, even Amanda. What would his new friends think if they saw Trino in a shelter like this? His family had no house, no food, no money—the little bit they had owned had been lost in the storm.

Trino sighed. He'd probably lose his friends, too, once Stephanie told them what she saw and "smelled" today. He pushed away the cereal bowl, and left the table.

As he returned to the row of cots where his family now lived, he saw his mother taking their "clean" clothes and packing them in two cardboard boxes.

"Are we leaving?"

"No. I just want to put things away. I noticed a little boy wearing a T-shirt that looks like one Gus had."

"Where?" Trino looked around, anxious to catch a thief who had taken what little they had left. He'd love to pound someone—anyone—at this moment. "Who is it?"

"What does it matter?" she said. "The shirt had a hole in it."

Trino sighed, wishing there was something to do besides think about how bad their life was right now. But he wasn't a little kid like Gus and Beto, who were happy to play wherever they were. And Félix had made friends who hung out on the bleachers and bragged about stuff that Trino knew was nothing but lies.

"¡Ay, Dios mío!" His mother's startled voice took Trino by surprise. He saw her hands move over her hair, smoothing out tangles and pressing it down with her fingers. "What is *he* doing here?"

Trino turned and immediately understood his mother's reaction.

Nick Longoria walked towards them. He wore a clean, white, buttoned shirt and black jeans. He stopped at the cot between Trino and his mom. His dark face was serious, his eyes taking in what he saw before him.

"Hello, María. Trino. Are you all right?"

She lowered her hands. They hung limp at her sides. "How did you find us, Nick?"

"I saw you on the TV news. You should have called me. I would have come for you and the boys."

"How could I call you? We don't have a phone," she answered.

Then Nick turned to stare at Trino. "Are you okay, son?"

"I'm fine. What do you want, Nick?" Only after he heard his words did Trino realize how cold he sounded. It was this place, everything he had been through, that made him sound like he wasn't glad to see Nick. But he really was.

Nick gave Trino one of those easy smiles he carried around with him like a comb in his pocket. "I came to check on you and your mother, Trino. With this storm, I'm going to have plenty of work for us to do. Are you ready?"

"I'd be stupid not to work with you," Trino replied, still uncertain why his voice sounded so ungrateful and cold. He shook his head, trying to clear it and think straight. "I tried to get us a job with Mr. Cummins cutting down the tree that hit our trailer, but he didn't want us."

Nick shrugged. "Sometimes the guy says no. It happens to me, too." He turned back to Trino's mom. "I'm proud of what Trino did to help you, María." He stepped forward and took her hands in his. "I'm glad nothing happened to you."

"Me, too." Her voice shook as she looked up at him. She swallowed with difficulty, then said, "How are you, Nick? Was the storm bad where you live?"

"The ground was so hard, the rain couldn't seep in. The water got high pretty fast, but it's going down now."

"That's good."

"Yeah, that's good."

"María—Nick—" They spoke at the same time.

Trino watched as Nick pulled her towards him, placing his arms around her shoulders, like he didn't want to break her. She slipped her arms around his waist. They seemed to melt together into one person.

Yesterday Trino had seen people hold one another, cry together, or find some awkward words to say. But what he saw in front of him gave him a glimpse of love, a feeling of hope. His family needed both. Was he ready to admit that he wanted it, too?

He had only admitted to himself in the past few days how much he missed Nick. At first, he missed earning twenty dollars when he worked with Nick. Now, he knew he missed a man he could talk to, a man who gave him some good advice without making a big speech like teachers did.

For the first time, Trino saw Nick kiss his mom. It wasn't one of those long, hungry kisses like characters in a *telenovela*, but a kiss that didn't embarrass a person to watch. It just made him think, *they must really like each other*. It didn't scare Trino or make him mad. Nick had returned because he cared about Trino's mom, and because he had some work for Trino. The storm had done some serious damage, but Trino didn't feel like everything was gone for good. He'd help his mom put their lives back together, and it looked like Nick would help them, too.

"Nick! Nick!" Gus and Beto had seen him and had run over from their games with the other children.

"Did you bring us any candy?" Beto asked, clinging to one of Nick's long legs.

Nick let go of their mother to lift Gus into his arms. He rubbed the top of Beto's head.

"I don't have candy, but I'll take you to my house. Do you want to see where I live?"

"Where you live?" Gus asked him, his little fingers searching the pockets of Nick's white shirt. "I want some gum, Nick."

"Nick, how can we go stay with you? How will the boys get to school? I need to be close by so Mala can watch the *niños*. I start my new job tomorrow." His mom's sudden smile made her look like a happy kid at a birthday party. "Nick, I got a job at the college."

He grinned and put his other arm around her shoulders. "I knew you could do it."

"I was so mean to you—I know you didn't break the TV—but I was scared to go there."

"What changed your mind?"

She looked towards Trino. "My son. Trino got food from Mr. Epifaño. He even tried to bring home a little money. And he did some stuff for school that got me thinking." She turned back towards Nick. "I wanted a better job. It was something I had to do for myself. And for my kids."

Nick lowered his face and kissed her lips. "I'm very proud of you, María. And I just know you're going to like working at the college."

"It'll be good to work at a place where you do, Nick." She reached up to stroke his cheek, then let her hand slip down Gus's squirming body. She patted her son's back. "You get down now. Nick and I need to make some plans. Go and play." She looked down at Beto.

"You, too, *vámonos!*" Then she gave Trino a look and a slight jerk of her head that meant *get lost.*

Trino walked off, wishing he could stick around and see what plans his mom had in mind.

He wouldn't mind living at Nick's place—wherever it was—but like his mother, Trino wanted to stick around the neighborhood. He wondered if they could stay here in the gym past tomorrow. The school would need the space for gym classes, wouldn't it?

He wandered towards the TV set, but there was just a football game and a bunch of older men watching it. He felt a nervous feeling inside him, like he had been inside this place too long. He looked behind him, saw Nick and his mom talking as they sat on a low bleacher near their cots. He wanted to walk outside by himself to think.

"Trino! We found you!"

The girl's voice was familiar, but Trino didn't want to think it could be her, coming inside a place like this. Slowly, he turned around to face not only Lisana, but also her brother Jimmy, Hector, Albert, and Amanda, too. His face flushed hot. They all looked so clean, and he felt like he had slept in his clothes, which he had, of course.

"We didn't know for sure if you'd still be here," Amanda said, glancing at Lisana, then giving Trino a slight smile.

"Wow," Hector said, turning his head to look around the gym. "Do they let you play B-ball all you want in here?"

"Yeah, right. He's going to dunk a basket and hit some old man in a cot, right?" Jimmy gave Hector a friendly shove. "Use your head, man."

Hector just laughed, then he gave Trino a shrug, tossing his hands up at his sides.

Trino found himself smiling, although his legs felt weak as he saw Lisana watching him. "Uh—why are you here, anyway?"

"We saw you on TV last night," Lisana said. "That tree looked just deadly. I'm glad you—and your mom—are okay."

"Were you scared, going inside the trailer with that tree on top of it?" Albert asked.

Trino shrugged. "I don't know. I was too busy to be scared, I guess."

"It's too bad about your house, man," Jimmy told Trino. "What are you going to do now?"

"I don't know," he said again, then realized he sounded dumb. "I mean—my mom hasn't made any real plans yet. I guess we'll stay with somebody—maybe my aunt—or one of her friends . . ."

His voice trailed off as he saw them looking around the gym, staring at the sight to which he had grown accustomed. It was noisy, crowded, and filled with messy people. Like his family, they had little money, no place to call a home, and didn't know what would happen next. These were clean kids from a nice neighborhood. What were they thinking about all this?

"Trino? I brought you a couple of candy bars." Amanda's voice was quiet as she extended him a small brown bag. "I know it's not much, but I thought you might enjoy them."

Trino took the bag from her, surprised by her kindness. "Uh—thanks—Amanda."

"Albert and I brought you some of our comic books. There's a real cool one with aliens that always makes me laugh," Hector said, as Albert handed him a short pile of colorful comic books.

"I brought you two T-shirts," Jimmy said, and gave Trino a white plastic grocery bag. "I heard on the TV that you didn't have any clothes. My sister, Abby, washed them and everything. We're about the same size, don't you think?"

"Sure, man, thanks," Trino said, but words were getting more difficult to say. He couldn't believe they had come to see him. They had even brought him stuff. What about that?

Lisana stepped forward and looked right into Trino's eyes. "I want to help you and your mom clean up the trailer. I can help after school—just let me know."

"Sure, Trino, I'll help, too," Amanda said. "Once we give the history reports tomorrow, we'll be free to help you anytime."

Hector gave Trino a friendly slug on the arm. "Yeah, man. Can you imagine how it's gonna be tomorrow when you and I stand up and tell everyone about José Antonio Navarro. I guess we ought to call you a *tejano* hero, too, huh?"

Trino's eyes widened as if Hector had just hit him in the stomach. The nauseous feeling grew stronger as Trino realized what else he had left behind in the trailer.

He recalled everything as if it had just happened. Yesterday, he had just dumped his books and folder on the sofa before he went to get Gus and Beto at Mala's house. He had tossed everything on the floor later when he tried to take a nap. How could he have been so stupid? And how was he going to tell his "partner" that their report was now a pile of mush under muddy waters in a trailer?

Chapter Fourteen
El tiempo hablará por todo

Trino had told many lies in his life to look cool, or to act tough, or just to save his butt. But he couldn't think of any lie that could save him now.

He looked at Hector, who wore the smiling face of somebody who had no idea that all his hard work was now just a pile of wet papers. Even if Trino tried to sneak back into the trailer again, he knew that what he found would be worthless. How could they give Coach a report that had been soaked by the rain falling through the hole in the bathroom ceiling?

It was Lisana who said, "Trino? Are you okay? Your face looks a little strange."

He glanced at Lisana first, then at Hector. He saw Jimmy, Albert, and Amanda staring at him. These kids had acted like his friends today—bringing him stuff. They had worked together on the history projects, too. What would they think of him when he told Hector the truth?

Trino took a deep breath, then eyed Hector directly. The feelings that churned inside him were a nauseous combination of disappointment and nervousness. He had no idea how Hector would take it.

"Hector, the report was at my house. It's flooded, man. The report's flooded, too."

"What? What are you telling me, Trino?"

"The report's gone, Hector. That's what I'm telling you. I left my books and stuff on the floor. When I went back inside, everything was flooded. Mud and water were everywhere."

Hector's face got red. "How could you be so stupid? Why didn't you just leave the report in your locker?"

"I took it home to read it over again."

"What!" Hector grabbed Trino's arms in a tight grip. "Why did you do that?"

"Let go of me!" Trino jerked his shoulder to get Hector's hands off of him. "You think I wanted this to happen?"

"Don't you get it? Coach said that the report's worth two test grades. If I flunk this, I'll never get off the bench and play ball."

"How can you be so selfish, Hector?" Lisana's voice was deep with anger. Her face looked mad enough to hit someone—maybe even Hector. "Trino's family's lost everything! And all you can think about is that you'll flunk and not be able to play basketball?"

"Lisana, wait—" Trino put his hand up near her shoulder. He knew Hector had a right to his feelings. "I know that Hector's pretty mad—I've been feeling mad for the last two days, so I know how he feels." He looked at his partner again. "Hector, I'm really sorry, man. I don't know what we can do except to write it all over again."

"By tomorrow? Are you crazy?" Hector sounded as if he was out of breath. "Man, I knew I should have kept the report. I just knew that something like this would happen."

"Yeah, right." Amanda gave Hector a roll of her eyes. "Like you knew a tree was going to fall on Trino's trailer, and the rain would come in and ruin your report. Get real, Hector! It was an accident."

"Yeah," Jimmy said. "Don't you think that Coach Treviño will understand — that it was an accident?"

"I think he will," Amanda said.

"Well, I don't!" Hector gave all of them an angry pass of his eyes. "I sit in front of the class. And I get to hear all the lame excuses that kids tell him. Do you really think he's going to listen when I tell him that the report got trashed in Trino's house when a tree came through the ceiling? It sounds crazy to me, and I even saw the mess on TV."

"Well, if Coach saw it on TV, too, then you'll probably be okay," Amanda answered.

Hector threw up his hands and walked away from all of them.

But Trino followed him. "Hector, this isn't just your project. It's mine, too. What happened is crappy, but somehow, we still get to do the report. Why can't we just *talk* about what we know? Think of Navarro. He walked into a room of *gringos* who couldn't even speak his language, and he said—"

"We aren't Navarro, Trino. We're just two kids without a history report." Hector spoke as if nothing would change his mind.

Trino lost his temper, then. "Man, you're just going to quit, aren't you? If I quit every time something didn't work out like I planned, I'd probably be dead like Zipper. But I'm not a quitter, Hector. And you're pretty stupid if you just give up and don't at least *try* to explain what happened to Coach Treviño. What have we got to lose?"

Hector just waved Trino off, and stomped out of the gym.

"Lisana's right. You're selfish. You're only thinking of yourself."

Now Trino had no report *and* no partner. He shook his head and turned back around to where the others stood, staring at him.

"Hector's being so stupid," Jimmy said.

Trino shrugged, and put a tighter grip on the bags that Amanda and Jimmy had given him. There was silence, as if no one knew what to say next.

"I guess we'd better go," Lisana said, shifting her weight from foot to foot. "We'll see you in school tomorrow."

"I don't know." Trino thought of facing Coach Treviño alone and slid right into a lie. "I'll probably have to watch my brothers so my mom can work."

"But the history reports start tomorrow," Amanda said.

"Yes, Trino." Lisana put her hand on Trino's arm. "You've got to talk to Coach. He'll probably let you turn it in late because of what happened."

"I don't know," Trino repeated, because he honestly couldn't tell if he'd go to school tomorrow. Even if his mother worked out something with Mala, Trino didn't know if he wanted to go back. Maybe he'd skip school a few days, then just tell Coach "I didn't do it."

What did it matter if he got a zero for his work? He'd gotten a lot of zeroes from teachers and nothing bad ever happened. They were just numbers on a page.

Trino said good-bye to his friends, remembered to thank them for what they had brought, then he walked to a door labeled "Boys." He sat by himself in the empty locker room.

For the long time that he sat there, Trino's thoughts spun around him like a web. When Zipper died, he blamed himself because he couldn't help his friend, couldn't stop the bullet that killed him. Zipper was dead; there was nothing left to do for him. But why couldn't he feel like there was nothing he could do about the stupid history report? Why did he feel like he had let another friend down?

Trino knew he had worked hard on the report, harder than he had ever worked at school to do something well. It showed who he was, and what he could do. He wanted to hang around with the guys and Lisana. He liked to be friends with them, having people to talk to and joke around with. He had lost so much since yesterday. He didn't want to lose his friends, too.

If he didn't go to school, didn't try to explain what happened to Coach, would he lose the respect he'd worked so hard to gain? He'd gotten others to accept him in a better way, and now wasn't the time to give up. He felt as if he was back on that old tree limb, inching his way across it. Even when the branch had broken, Trino had held tight, had gotten himself back to safe ground. He couldn't let go, stop trying, just give up. Not now.

He had no idea how long he stayed in the locker room. When he came out, he was surprised to see Mr. Cummins talking to his mother and Nick. He didn't know what to expect, but at least everyone was smiling.

"We have a place to live again," Trino's mom said when she saw him. "Mr. Cummins has a small trailer behind his that we can use for the next month. Since I had just paid him the rent money, he thought it was only fair."

"It'll give you a few weeks to make some plans. Maybe we can repair the roof of your trailer by then," Mr. Cummins said. Then he took a step towards Trino. "Listen, son, I've been thinking about what you said outside the trailer. You said that you work with a man who cuts down trees. I sure could use you to clean up a couple of spots where branches fell. But I'm also worried about a couple of dead trees in the lot. Another good wind and they'll be down on somebody's house, too. What does your man charge?"

Trino glanced at Nick, who just gave him a nod of his chin. He took it to mean that it was up to Trino to set a price. He could get some decent money if Nick stuck to their bargain. And Trino had a good feeling that Nick was a man who stood behind his handshake.

"We usually get about seventy-five dollars a tree," Trino said. "We charge extra if you want us to haul it to the dump. An extra twenty—to pay for the gas."

"That's pretty reasonable, Trino. Can you ask the man to call me soon?"

Trino smiled, feeling very pleased with himself. "He's right here." He gestured towards Nick. "Nick and I work together, Mr. Cummins."

"Oh, I didn't realize—I guess I should have asked *you* for a price." Mr. Cummins looked from Trino to Nick and stepped backwards to face the taller man.

"No, Trino gave you our price. You can trust him," Nick said, and placed his hand on Trino's shoulder. "He does a good job cutting down trees, Mr. Cummins. I know you'll be satisfied."

"What's in your bag, Trino?" Beto suddenly asked. The little boy poked his fingers at the brown bag Trino held by his side.

Trino felt so good inside that he smiled at his brother. "It's some candy, Beto. My friends brought us some candy to eat. Do you want some?"

Not long after Mr. Cummins left, Mala came into the gym. She had seen them on TV and offered them her spare bedroom. "And of course, I'll watch the boys when you start your new job."

Then his mom's family showed up. Tía Sofia and Tío Felipe had seen the TV news, too. They came with two bags of groceries, some towels, a mop, and a broom. They also offered Trino's family a place to live.

Trino's mom said a lot of "thank yous" but told Nick, Mala, and her family, "We'll make a home as best we can at the trailer park and start again. I think we're ready now."

<hr />

Trino ran hard.

His mother had left early with Gus and Beto. She had told Trino to get up for school, but he had just turned over for one more minute of sleep. When he opened his eyes again, a stab of panic told him he had slept too long. He ran to the kitchen to see the wall clock that Mr. Cummins had put up above the refrigerator. Eight-thirty. He shook Félix as he yelled,

"Wake up!"

His little brother looked at him through sleepy eyes. "Huh?"

"You're on your own, man. I got to go." He didn't care if his brother stayed asleep all day as he threw on his clothes, wet down his hair, and left his shoes untied as he ran to school.

He had wanted to get to school early, talk to Hector, talk to Coach. Last night he had gone over what he would say to both of them, what he would say about José Antonio Navarro, and what he wanted to tell Lisana, Jimmy, and Amanda when he saw them at lunch. Everything was just a jumbled mess in his head now as he ran to school.

The school office was in a crazy state of confusion, and it just made Trino later. There weren't enough substitutes for teachers who had gone to some meeting. Parents were there trying to get new books to replace those damaged by flooded houses. Students who were late were trying to get tardy slips. The secretary seemed to be yelling at everyone.

As the secretary finally handed Trino his tardy slip, the bell to end second period rang loudly in the office.

Trino ran again, this time to reach Coach Treviño's class to talk to him. Only it was Hector that Trino saw first.

The big kid looked like he had just eaten something he didn't like. His face was puckered together and his hands pressed on his stomach. He stood outside the door of Coach Treviño's classroom.

"Trino! There you are!" Hector straightened up, but his face didn't change. "I was afraid you'd skip out today."

"I slept too long, that's all. So, what's up?" Trino got right to the point. "Are *you* going to skip out or stand with me when I talk to Coach?" He didn't break eye contact with Hector. "I can give my half of the report best as I can from memory. What about you?"

Slowly, Hector's face loosened up. He took a deep breath, and said, "I guess we have no choice, do we?" He gave Trino a little grin. "If only we had a hundred dollars to slip Coach, too."

Trino raised an eyebrow. "Yeah, right."

Both boys laughed a little then.

"Actually, we're not completely lost." Hector pulled some papers from his folder. "I found some of our old notes from the college library. I recopied what I could—it will help, I think, if we get stuck and forget what to say next."

"That's good, Hector. At least it's something." Trino glanced down to see some of his own handwriting on some of the old notes and Hector's neater handwriting on other papers. He felt better to have the proof of their attempts to do the work in his own hands.

"Trino, about yesterday—" Hector's voice shook a little. "I'm sorry I was such a jerk. I just wanted us to do good on this report—and I was just so mad."

Trino nodded, then said, "Come on, *partner*. Let's go tell Coach what happened."

Together they walked into the classroom. Coach Treviño was talking to two girls at his desk. Only a handful of other students sat in desks in the classroom.

"Well, just do the best you can, ladies," he was saying. "I told you there were no excuses. You either have the report for me, or it's a pair of zeroes for both of you."

At those words, Hector stopped. His face looked as if they were again stuck in the janitor's closet with no way out. Trino paused, saw Hector's face, and grabbed his arm. Trino pulled him along as he took a couple steps closer to Coach Treviño's desk.

"Coach, we need to talk to you about our report," Trino said, pushing the words from his mouth, even though his throat was dry and his jaw felt stiff.

The man turned to them and rolled his eyes. "Not you, too? All I've heard today are excuses. Why can't just one of you come up and say, 'Gosh, Coach, my partner and I are all ready for this report.' Didn't anyone do this assignment right?"

Trino frowned, trying to ignore the frustration and sarcasm in his teacher's voice.

"Coach, Hector and I did the assignment, remember? We even went to the college library and got extra notes for our report." He took a deep breath, then said, "I took the report home with me, but it got messed up. I know this is going to sound lame and stupid, but the truth is, a tree fell on top of my trailer. It busted a hole in the ceiling, and rain came in and ruined everything."

"Coach, didn't you see Trino's trailer on TV?" Hector interrupted with his own way of explaining what had happened. "It was a big mess! But Trino—he went back inside to get his mom's clothes and stuff, 'cause they had nothing to wear when they went to the shelter. Trino was on TV and everything."

Coach Treviño nodded and said, "So you have no report—"

"No, we have a report to give the class," Trino said. "We just don't have one to give you. Hector and I need to rewrite it, Coach." He turned and looked at his partner.

"We're going to be just like José Antonio Navarro," Trino said. "He walked into a room full of *gringos* with only his words to help him. Hector and I have just our words, too."

Both boys turned back to look at their teacher.

Hector stood up straight, pressing his shoulders back. "Trino's family lost everything this weekend, Coach. I mean *everything*. I felt mad when I heard that our report got trashed at Trino's house. But I've been thinking a lot since yesterday. Trino is here, ready to be my partner, and we're going to do the best we can with this report. We worked too hard on it to quit now. Right, Trino?"

"Right, Hector." At that moment, Trino realized no matter what, Hector was still going to be his friend. The others had proved to be his friends, too. That raw feeling of loneliness Trino had carried around for the past few months seemed to fade out like an old scar.

"Coach, I'm the one who screwed up," Trino said. "Don't give Hector a zero because of me."

Coach Treviño looked at Trino, then at Hector. By now his face had relaxed, and his lips seemed to be holding back a smile. "I admit, you two surprised me. I saw Trino on TV, and I knew what had happened to his family. I didn't even think you'd come to school, Trino. And Hector—I'm proud that you're not laying blame on Trino and crying about it. You're standing up together and still plan to do the report. Well, I don't know what it is about José Antonio Navarro that's got you two so fired up, but I can't wait to hear whatever you've got to say." He placed one hand on Trino's shoulder and another hand on Hector's. "You can have until next Monday to turn in a written report, okay?" He dropped his hands and then turned towards Trino. "Trino, let's talk after school today. Maybe the athletes can do a fundraiser to help your family out."

A surge of gratitude made Trino smile at the man. He had never had a teacher who made him feel like he mattered. He spoke his words slowly because they were so important. "Thanks, Coach—for giving us extra time—and for offering to help my family, too—thanks."

≈ ≈ ≈

Trino watched Will and Tim as they gave their report about Ben Milam. Everything they said sounded like it was copied straight from an encyclopedia. Vanessa and Yvette were next. Their report on Jane Long was more interesting because they kept repeating the line "and Jane Long waited," as they talked about her waiting for her husband, waiting for the War of Texas Independence to end, and waiting for other events in her life. Soon every-one in the class started to say the four words with them.

"You can tell they're cheerleaders," Hector whispered to Trino after the two girls had finished. "Cheerleaders always say the same thing over and over."

He smiled a little before they listened to the next report on Samuel McCullough, a free black man who fought in the Texas Revolution, too. The two boys who gave the report had very little to say, and Coach told them he was disappointed that they hadn't worked very hard to find more information about the man.

When Coach called on Trino and Hector to do their report next, Trino was nervous, but he knew that he and Hector had more information than the last boys, and knew they wouldn't be reading from papers like the first boys. It helped that he wasn't the only one to stand up in front of everyone and talk. Hector was usually a big talker, and Trino was depending on him to get the report going.

Trino followed Hector up to the front of the class. When they took their place behind Coach's wooden podi-um, Trino could feel the blood inside him rushing down his legs, making them tremble. Someone beat a drum in his ears, his stomach felt like he had just got off a dizzy ride, and his throat felt like it was going to close up.

He looked out at the twenty students staring at them, at Coach Treviño sitting in the back in his teacher's chair with an open notebook across his lap. What did they want from him? What did he have to offer?

"Trino and I are here to tell you about José Antonio Navarro," Hector said in a voice that was calm and confi-dent. "He was one of only two *tejanos* who signed the Texas Declaration of Independence. And we think that's a very cool thing."

Trino looked at his friend Hector, and felt a slight smile pull at his mouth. Time will speak for everything. Today he really understood what Navarro had meant.

Epilogue
Saturday, June 7

The last time Trino remembered standing so still was when that black snake had crawled out of the old tree trunk behind Mr. Cummins' trailer. He had been scared stiff. Why would he think of that now? He wasn't scared, just nervous about this new job he had.

Trino looked at Nick, whose face seemed relaxed. He spotted the tiny beads of sweat across the man's forehead. Maybe Nick was a little nervous about his new job, too. The guy wasn't just getting a wife, but gaining four sons, too. Was he ready for the change? Was Trino?

He liked Nick, sure, but Nick could be bossy, especially when it came to washing dishes after supper and doing school work. He also had a thing for reading newspapers, and expected them to listen to articles he read. Trino thought they were boring, and when he told Nick so, Nick said, "Then you must be a boring person 'cause you never learn anything new." Nick didn't like anyone to mess with his tools, and he made Trino stay home on Fridays so he and Trino's mom could go out. Trino had missed some fun times with his friends because of "Mama's Night Out," as Nick called it.

Yet, as Trino stood beside Nick in the small chapel, waiting as best man, he had to admit that having Nick

166

around had its good points. Even though Mr. Epifaño didn't need Trino, Nick kept him working. The past eight months, Nick had taught him about fixing engines when the truck broke down three times on the way to the city dump. Nick had let Trino drive the truck about five miles when they had gone to Perales to pick up a sofa and chairs from Nick's brother. And when his mom acted stubborn and unreasonable, Nick was often on Trino's side. Because of Nick, Trino usually had a couple of dollars in his pocket, he had shoes that didn't have holes, and now he wouldn't have to share a bedroom with his brothers anymore. Nick and Trino had remodeled the attic in Nick's house so Trino could have his own room. Best of all, when they moved into Nick's house, Trino wouldn't have to change schools.

"You're so lucky," Lisana had told him close to Christmas as they walked home together. They were alone because Jimmy had basketball practice and Lisana's girlfriends were riding the bus that day. He had taken her hand, and she squeezed his gently while she talked.

"When my mom died, and we had to live with Abby and Earl, I had to change schools and leave all my old friends behind." Then she turned her face up towards his. She gave him a smile that sent a rush of good feeling through him. "But if I was still at my old school, then I wouldn't know you, would I? I guess I'm a lucky person, too."

She stopped walking. Her face had turned very serious. "You know, Trino, I think of you as my very best friend. You know things about me that no one else does. How come I tell you so much?"

"I don't know, Lisana." He looked into her brown eyes and thought, *You are so pretty.* She was smart in school and one of those people that everyone liked. They had met by chance, but she never stopped being friendly to him. Why?

"You know why we're such good friends?" She seemed to be reading his mind. "You're a good listener. You just let me talk. You're not like Jimmy, who thinks most of what I say is dumb. You don't make fun of me like Hector and Albert do. Janie and Amanda talk so much, I don't think they ever listen. But you do. I can tell it in your eyes. Every time I talk, I see your eyes on me, and I know you're listening."

Trino swallowed. He did listen, but he kept his eyes on Lisana because he loved to look at her pretty face. Okay, so he cared about her, too. It was different from the way he felt about his mom, his brothers, or even Nick. He knew Hector, Jimmy, and Albert were his good friends—they had helped a lot when the trailer had to be cleaned up, and they had fun playing video games together. He had gotten used to Janie, and Amanda was okay most of the time. But Lisana was very special—just because she was Lisana.

"I know what you mean. You are my best friend, too," Trino said.

As they stood on the sidewalk, holding hands and facing each other with the truth, Trino remembered last night when Nick and his mom talked by the truck. Nick was holding her hand just as Trino held Lisana's now. Nick had leaned down and kissed Trino's mom, and she had smiled at him. He had never seen his mom's face look so happy. Because of Nick, his mom was less angry, and she laughed more often.

Lisana had done the same for Trino. He wanted to show Lisana how much he cared. And that's when he kissed Lisana for the very first time. He remembered every second, from her surprised gasp to the taste of her cherry lipstick on his lips when it was over.

A gentle poke in the ribs brought Trino back from the past. This memory always left a smile on his face. His smile got bigger as he saw Tía Reenie walking down the middle aisle towards the altar where Nick and Trino stood. Her short yellow dress made her look like a giant duck in spiked gold heels.

But Trino's mom looked like a white dove in her lace dress. It floated around her legs as she walked down the aisle of the little church in Perales. His little brothers sat in the front row with Tía Sofia and Tío Felipe. Other aunts and uncles, a few cousins, and some of Nick's family sat in the short wooden pews watching everything. He saw a little wave from Lisana, who sat about five rows back with Jimmy, their big sister Abby, and her husband Earl, who was holding on to little Nelda. The toddler looked like she wanted to come down the aisle, too.

Trino watched his mom walk up to meet Nick. Both of them took their place in front of a short gray-haired preacher named Mr. Sánchez, who had known Nick since he was a boy.

He felt his toes wiggle around in the black boots he had borrowed from Nick. In another year, they'd fit better. He probably looked like a schoolboy dressed in a white shirt, but at least no one asked him to wear a tie. They had just bought Trino new pants, and he had used one of his uncle's dress shirts. Nick wore a white *guayabera* shirt because he wanted to keep it simple. Yet, when it came to Trino's mom, he insisted she get a new white dress "as pretty as you want because I want my bride to be the most beautiful woman in the church."

His eyes wandered over towards his mom and Nick, then he started to listen to the preacher talk about good times and bad times, sick times and healthy times. Times with no money and times with plenty to eat.

Trino thought, *it sounds like my life.* Only he had little time to think more about it because the preacher asked for the wedding ring. He extended his hand towards Trino. Nick raised an eyebrow, and his mom chewed on her lip as they looked at the best man.

Trino fumbled with his shirt pocket because his hands shook. The shirt material was slick and his fingers slid around inside the pocket. He felt sweaty by the time he gave the gold ring with two small diamonds to the preacher.

Trino licked his lips and wiped his sweaty hands down his pants legs. Then he relaxed because the most important part of the job was over. He could stand by Nick and his mom now, and just think about the party and all the good food waiting at Nick's brother's house. He couldn't wait to change back to his jeans and T-shirt and feel like himself again.

He listened to the preacher call them man and wife. He saw Nick turn and kiss his mom like he really meant it. Everybody in the chapel laughed, even Trino. And that was the moment Trino decided that if Nick was ready for a change, then he was, too.

About the Author

Diane Gonzales Bertrand was born in San Antonio, Texas, in a Westside neighborhood that serves as the setting for many of her books. She is the middle daughter in a family of seven children. She attended Little Flower School and Ursuline Academy. She earned college degrees from the University of Texas at San Antonio (B.A. 1979) and Our Lady of the Lake University (M.A. 1992). She wrote her first novel in fifth grade and continued to write poems, plays, and stories to share with her family and friends. She taught both middle school and high school and is currently Writer-In-Residence at St. Mary's University, where she teaches creative writing and English composition.

In a family of seven children, reading library books was an inexpensive entertainment. Reading inspired Diane to write her own stories, especially when she noticed few books featured Hispanic lead characters. Thus she wrote three romantic novels for Avalon Books with Hispanic heroines. Arte Público Press published her novel *Sweet Fifteen* (1995) and an intermediate grade novel, *Alicia's Treasure* (1996). She wrote about her family in her bi-lingual picture books *Sip, Slurp, Soup, Soup/Caldo, caldo, caldo* (1997) and *Family, Familia* (1999). She took on the challenge of writing for middle school readers in the award winning *Trino's Choice* (1999) and its sequel *Trino's Time*. New picture books include *The Last Doll* (2000) and *Uncle Chente's Picnic* (2001).

She still lives in San Antonio with her husband, Nick, and their two teenage children, Nick G. and Suzanne.